[untitled]

issue six

Pinion Press
2/118 Para Road
Montmorency, Victoria
Australia 3094
www.busybird.com.au

Pinion Press is an imprint of Busybird Publishing

First published by Busybird Publishing 2014
Copyright © 2014 remains with the contributors

Cover artwork and illustrations: Kev Howlett
Layout: Les Zigomanis
Chief Editor: Les Zigomanis
Assistant Editors: Blaise van Hecke, Daniel Kovacevic, Jodie Garth, Helen Krionas, Lisa Roberts, and Danielle Gori
Proofreaders: Terri Giuretis, Erin Harvey, Ariel Skippen
International Ambassador: Isolde Martin

Typeset in Adobe Garamond Pro 11pt

ISBN 9780992432515
ISSN 1836-9065

This book is copyright. Apart from any fair dealing for the purposes of study, research, criticism, review, or as otherwise permitted under the Copyright Act, no part may be reproduced by any process without written permission. Enquiries should be made through the publisher.

Busybird Publishing
2/118 Para Road
Montmorency Victoria
Australia 3094
www.busybird.com.au

Busybird Publishing s a proud member of the Small Press Network (SPN): www.spunc.com.au.

Contents

Editorial

Where has *[untitled]* been?

That is a question you're perfectly entitled to ask.

And here is the answer: I'm not telling.

Okay, the publisher has just brutally nudged me with her boot, so I guess some explanation is in order.

Usually, *[untitled]* would come out around about March or April of every year. Or September. Possibly November. Well, every year at least. We haven't missed a year since 2009 – not a huge streak by any means, but a streak all the same. What's more, it was an unbroken streak.

Unfortunately, we can't say that again.

2013 was the first year that went by – zipped by, like an elephant snowboarding – without an *[untitled]* being published. Many might've thought we'd gone on a sabbatical. Or folded under the pressures of the demanding publishing industry. Or gambled away our meagre funds. Or maybe just forgotten about all of you.

Of course, that could never happen. We don't have any funds to gamble away.

Nor would we – or could we – ever forget *you*, the reader, who helps make *[untitled]* possible. And whilst

2013 went by without an *[untitled]*, we were still working industriously on issue six, striving to meet a deadline that continued to be nudged further and further along until, somehow, it tripped over, fell into 2014, and crawled all the way into February, sputteringly triumphant.

If you've been a regular reader of *[untitled]* (or our blog on the Busybird website), you would've read ad nauseam how we just want to be about stories – stories that are good reads. We don't care what genre those stories are. Look back at previous issues, and we've had contemporary fiction, sci-fi, horror, satire, comedy, and the list goes on. What all the stories have had in common is their capacity to entertain and the strength of the voice of the author.

That's another thing we love to bang on about: voice. It's the way the author *sounds* – at least figuratively – when you read a story. Every author has a voice that is unique to them. Even if they attempt to change styles, if they change genre, if they write backwards, their voice is at the heart of their stories. Analogously, think of the immortal *Bohemian Rhapsody* (yes, mama mia, it's immortal, damnit) by Queen and the vocal range of Freddie Mercury. He hits high notes, he hits low notes, he sings the song as a ballad, he sings it as rock, he's capable of constantly sounding different, but at the heart of it all is Freddie's powerful and unique voice. You can always tell it no matter *how* it sounds.

Perhaps it's this observation of (or is it *obsession with*) voice that has delayed this little *[untitled]*, as we've ploughed through stories – more stories than ever, in fact (and not by a little way, but by a *looooonnnnnng* way) – searching, searching, *searching,* until ending with the selection of stories that you're holding now in your hands.

Because in producing *[untitled]*, we do have a dream. Initially, we wanted to create a market that also helped promote more mainstream and/or pop fiction, not to mention promoting new and emerging authors. But we also wanted to be recognised as a good little book of fiction.

Think about that: *[untitled] is* a literary journal. There's no doubt about that. We are a market for writers. The bulk of our readers are likely to be writers. But we want to evolve beyond that. We want to become an annual anthology of fiction that *also* the everyday reader will seek out and enjoy, and that collectors will, well, collect.

Far-fetched, possibly, but we're a book of short stories. There are other books of short stories out there, and maybe it's time to forget the archetype of *just* being a journal, to being identified *as* a journal, and to become that something more.

A book.

Of course, we could never do that without all of you — contributors (successful and unsuccessful), readers, interns, assistant editors, and our publishers. In fact, I am the only one unthanked. (sad-smiley-face.jpg, Mr Printer — *what do you mean there's no jpg? That's it, you're off the list!*)

In any case, for your patience, your tolerance, and your investment, we all here thank you with sincerity and humility.

Hope you enjoy what lies ahead. And if you're wondering, to make up for the absence of an *[untitled]* in 2013, there'll be two issues (hopefully) in 2014.

(Or at least we hope.)

The Stench of Adventure

Josh Donellan

The *Friends* theme song echoes around the lobby. Reeking of the profound filth that one can only absorb on a Cambodian night bus, I approach the front desk. A surly teenager hands me my keys, points upstairs and says, 'Number 25? You understand? 25?' His eyes are inexorably fixed on the flickering screen in front of him. Nasal American voices and canned laughter taunt me as I lug my backpack and laptop awkwardly up the narrow staircase. I dump my gear in my predictably appalling room and collapse onto the bed, tracing the cracks in the ceiling with my eyes.

The room is thick with that ubiquitous budget accommodation aroma of sweat, mould and tears. I'm surprised some enterprising perfumer hasn't tried to bottle it for the nostalgic forty-somethings wanting to relive their romanticised youth. I can just see some chiselled, Nordic blonde standing in front of a tropical sunset whispering, '*WANDERLUST: the stink of freedom, the stench of adventure ... by Calvin Klein.*'

It's been over a week since I've had a decent night's sleep, and twice as long since I've made any progress on my novel – ostensibly the reason for this trip in the first place. I'd told my friends I was going to travel so I could be like Hemingway: drink heavily and write like a genius. I got one part right.

For a few minutes my writer's guilt, the need to cleanse, and the desire for sleep battle for dominance. I put an end to the conflict by changing my shirt, descending the stairs, and stepping out into the blistering Cambodian sun.

The streets of Kratie are filled with motorcycles, vendors and, of course, tourists. Kratie is also home to the famous Irrawaddy dolphins, making it an essential part on the itinerary of anyone making the trip from Cambodia into southern Laos. The town itself is an eyesore, so it's rare for anyone to stay longer than a single evening. It's the city that everyone wants for a one-night stand.

I'm about to go in search of a bar when a tuk-tuk screeches to a halt in front of me and a man in a red baseball cap declares, 'Hey! You want dolphin tour? I take you, no problem! Okay get in!' The driver has a manic, mirthful energy. He reminds me of an Asian version of Flava Flav.

'Can we pick up beers on the way?'

He grins as he reaches between his feet and produces a large bottle of Angkor beer. I grab the bottle from him and clamber into the back of his tuk-tuk. He tells me his name is Ricky, which I can only assume is the abbreviated alteration of his Khmer name that he employs for dumb white tourists such as myself. Over the roar of his two-stroke engine, Ricky regales me with stories about his family, life in Kratie and bedding an obese American woman.

'She was fat! Very fat! But I still make love on her!' he proclaims joyfully.

I take an immediate shine to Ricky. It's refreshing to converse with a local rather than someone who views all of Asia as a cut-price hedonistic theme park.

Ricky takes us to the temple first, parks his tuk-tuk and says, 'Okay! You go looking! I stay here, read book for make practise English. You come back one hour, no problem!'

I climb the several hundred stairs that lead up to the temple and am greeted by a stunning array of Cambodian architecture, Buddhist iconography and spectacular views of the Mekong, where I assume my dolphin friends await me with some kind of Disney-esque celebratory montage of synchronised dancing, song and fireworks.

I take my time studying the temple and nod at a few monks who grin and give me a thumbs up. I return the gesture and one of them pulls a face at me before laughing and running back towards the monastery, gleefully giggling. I continue walking around the temple, passing a dreadlocked girl who fixes me with disconcertingly unblinking eyes. Her face appears to have been treated by the same spiritual Botox as so many other westerners who come to Asia to study Buddhism, limiting their repertoire of expressions to profound concentration and condescending smile.

I wave awkwardly and continue to the peak of the mountain, then sit and gaze out at the river snaking through the landscape below. After ten minutes of perfect stillness, a sleek shape pierces the surface and then disappears. A moment later it re-emerges, this time with company.

Eager for my chance to see the dolphins up close, I jog back down the ancient stone steps and find Ricky smoking and chatting with some other tuk-tuk drivers and a wizened old monk. I can't follow the bulk of their conversation, but the international gesture for *She Had Really Huge Boobs* translates effectively. Ricky gets to the punch-line and they explode with laughter.

'Okay! Very nice, yes? Now see dolphins!' Ricky revs the strident, spluttering engine and I climb into the cab of the tuk-tuk. As we hurtle down the narrow dirt road Ricky entertains me with a few stories of various tourists he has met, musing on how strange it is that they all come and stay for just one night, never giving themselves time to really see the city or meet local people.

'How long you stay?' he asks.

'Ah … three nights. This is my third night, I leave tomorrow,' I say, feeling guilty even as the lie vomits out of my stupid mouth.

'Oh! Very good. Three nights and only just now come see dolphins?' He sounds bemused, but not suspicious.

'Yes. I was … busy writing.'

'Oh! You are writer?'

'Yes. Well, you know, most of the time.'

'You write about my country, about Cambodia?'

'Actually, not in this book. But maybe in the future.'

'Hey! That very good! Maybe you write story about me? Tell everyone how I make love on big fat American woman?'

'Well, yes, that is quite a tale …'

'Yeah! Good story. You tell everyone in your country!'

We arrive at the riverside and bundle in with a charming Swedish couple who look like they have just emerged from the pages of an Ikea ad, stopped at a North Face clearance sale, and landed here on the banks of the Mekong. They don't talk much, but judging by their excited grins they are happy to be here.

The boat takes us across the water, the breeze playing across its surface, partially alleviating the stifling humidity. The Swedes have their SLRs held ready like photographic snipers hoping to capture perfect moments in tiny 6x4 inch prisons. I take out my crappy pocket Pentax and brag about how I won it in a national writing competition (conveniently leaving out it was second prize, and that first went to a girl who wrote a terrible poem about her ovaries).

We wait in patient silence – well, at least the Swedes and I do. Ricky and the boat driver smoke and chat and occasionally point at us and laugh in what I hope is a friendly display of affection rather than ridicule. Finally, a dorsal fin breaks the surface, and the excited snapping of shutters commences. The Irrawaddy dolphins are every bit as strange and beautiful as I had hoped. The curious blunt snout gives the dolphin a permanently mischievous expression.

Two others soon join the first. The Swedes' cameras continue clacking as the dolphins dive and splash, surprisingly comfortable with having humans so close, especially considering that so many of their parents and grandparents have been slaughtered. The guide tells us the reason they are now so rare in this area is because the Khmer Rouge used to shoot them for target practice, as if they were trying to acquire vast quantities of bad Karma as rapidly as possible.

We spend twenty minutes snapping photos and waving adoringly at the dolphins, who spend the same amount of time diving and dancing and laughing. The boat takes us back to the shore, the Swedes jabbering as they trawl through their photos, indulging in the instant nostalgia that's commonplace amongst so many travellers. However, given the rare opportunity to catch these dolphins on film (or pixel, as the case may be), you'd have to be far more of a jerk than I am to begrudge them their excitement.

Ricky takes me back into town and asks me a few questions about life in Australia, girls and writing. He finds my answers hilarious no matter what they are, whether I'm talking about my dad's financial troubles, my girlfriend's alternatingly amusing and troubling penchant for drinking and yelling, or the prevalence of racism in Australian politics.

He drops me back at the hotel and high fives me as he says, 'Okay! See you! I look forward to read you stories!'

Despite never having taken my full name or contact details, he's charmingly convinced that this is an event that will inevitably transpire. I return to my room and spend the next hour half-heartedly scribbling notes for my novel, which I will *definitely* start serious work on in the next few days. Next week at the latest.

Eventually a combination of hunger and the desire to remove myself from the corrosive stench of my room draws me out into the street in search of food. A food-cart vendor waves at me and says, 'Hello, friend! You want try some?' I inspect his various offerings, all of which can be divided into *Things That May Or May Not Be Rats (On Sticks)* and *You Don't Even WANT to Know What That Is (On a Stick)*.

I head toward one of the little restaurants that adorn the edge of the river, grab a beer and am about to order a non stick-based meal when I hear a tuk-tuk beeping. I turn around to see a familiar red cap and beaming grin.

'Hey, Ricky, how are you?'

'Very good, my friend!' He's so excited to see me, you'd think it'd been a year since our first meeting. 'Hey, you want see dolphins?'

A disappointed frown invades my face. He doesn't even remember me. I shouldn't be saddened, but realising that I'm just another in a long line of fares, forgotten sixty minutes later, is more than a little depressing.

'Ricky, I already saw the dolphins – this morning, remember?'

He pulls a face at me like I've just asked him if he knows that water is wet and should therefore not be poured on electrical appliances, suede shoes or cats, and says, 'You come again, Josh! This time no charge. We go swimming!'

It's a weird invitation, but fits with one of my travel rules: Never say 'no' to an offer unless it's likely to end in grievous bodily harm or boredom.

'I have two tourists coming! Pretty girls from England!'

'Sure, why the hell not?'

I climb into the back of his tuk-tuk with beer in hand and we travel a few blocks to a mid-range hotel that is nothing short of palatial compared to my current residence. As two cute, blonde girls in shorts and bikini tops climb into the back of our little motorcycle chariot and we cruise down the highway, I can't help feeling like I'm in an Asian karaoke rip-off of a Jay-Z film clip.

Jenny and Kylie introduce themselves and we do the usual tourist exchange of data (*whereyoufrom? whereyoubeen? whereyouheadingtonext? howlongyoutravellingfor?* etc.). We start at the temple before heading back down to the river. When we reach the water's edge, Ricky introduces us to a diminutive man with a spasmodically-toothed grin.

'Okay, you girls go with my friend. His name Phirun. I come back soon. You see dolphin, okay?'

'Aren't you coming with us?' Jenny asks, directing the question more to me than Ricky.

'Ah … no … we have to go … to … a … place?' I reply. I've never been good at lying. Well, that's not true; I'm an excellent liar when I'm allowed to sit down at a computer and obsessively edit my elaborate deceptions. In the flesh I'm about as convincing as a third grade performance of *Macbeth*.

The girls wave and hop into the boat, their perplexed expressions fading into the distance as the boat speeds up the river. Ricky grins and says, 'Okay! Now we go swimming! Come, come!'

'Why aren't the girls coming with us?'

Ricky scrunches up his face in bemusement and says, 'This special place. Not for strangers, only for friends.'

I follow him to the tuk-tuk and he drives just a few blocks to another bend in the river, where a rickety series of makeshift bathing platforms have been cobbled together with a handful of nails and some haphazardly tied rope. Families are camped at the various platforms, lounging around, smoking, swimming. They regard us with a sort of apathetic curiosity.

Ricky and I walk through the platforms. He swaps a few quick salutations with the bathers, and finally we reach a sand dune on the other side.

'We aren't swimming at the platforms?' I ask.

Ricky grins and replies, 'No! Dolphins no come to platforms.'

He picks up pace and races ahead over the dune. I follow him into a secluded little spot completely hidden from human eyes, save the tourist boats barely discernible in the distance.

'Okay! Now we swim!' He strips off down to his jocks and waits for me to do the same. This is a problem for two reasons. One: I'm incredibly self-conscious about my physique. Not quite 'Hey, baby, let's leave the lights off and my shirt on tonight', but not too far off that either. Two: My wallet and camera are going to have to go in this little pile of clothes.

What if this whole thing has been an elaborate con? I imagine myself running through the outskirts of Kratie, clad in nothing but wet boxers, getting snapped by some tourist and ending up as the centrepiece of some hideous internet meme with a title like OH NO FORGOT

PANTZ! There's no way to live that kind of thing down; I hear the infamous 'Star Wars Kid' is still in therapy.

'Why you no come swim?' asks Ricky, splashing around and grinning. I consider asking him if he knows what an internet meme is, but instead strip down and dive into the water. I keep my eyes trained on the dunes, waiting to see some shifty stranger appear and pocket my wallet and camera, but there is only the gentle sound of the water and the soft peach and pink hues of the setting sun. It is that rare flavour of beauty that can only be experienced as a stranger in a strange land.

Ricky splashes me and giggles. He must eat a bowl of childlike wonder every day for breakfast. I envy his uncomplicated, confident glee and wish I could dump my multitudinous neuroses out of my head and just fill it with joy. I am equally aware that given the choice, Ricky would trade lives with me in an instant.

I catch a ripple in the periphery of my vision and turn to see a pair of curious dolphins breaking the surface of the water mere metres away. Ricky grins so widely I'm worried the top half of his head is going to fall off. I stare at these two rare, unusual creatures, as they jump, carouse and sing.

It lasts only a few minutes, and with my camera well out of reach I have no means of transcribing this moment, save on the imperfect parchment of my memory. This is an experience that will return to me on my deathbed as I look back over the joys of my life, starting with my Optimus Prime cake on my fourth birthday and presumably concluding with becoming the first nonagenarian to parachute naked from a helicopter. Somewhere in between those two bookending raptures, this moment right here will feature prominently in the catalogue of experiences that have made this life worth living.

Ricky and I say nothing to each other, just stare and exchange disbelieving grins. And then the dolphins are gone.

'Very lucky to see dolphins so close!' exclaims Ricky, before tackling me under the water.

That night, sitting in my filthy hotel room, I stare at my laptop and try to will the words that will change the world to enter my head, but am instead faced with the shitty reality of my obstreperous cursor blinking back at me. I lie back on the mattress and stare at the rickety fan spinning around the ceiling.

An Open Book

Ryan O'Neill

The Front Cover

The front cover of the book shows a black and white photograph of an old man under the title, '**One Man's Folly: A Novel**'. The man has a round, bald head and wide-set eyes that have sleep in their corners. His wide mouth has a peculiar, twisted expression; one half of him appears to be smiling and the other half frowning.

Behind the old man can be seen part of a wall, against which hang dozens of glass cases containing butterflies, all of them carefully labelled with minute handwriting on small, oblong cards. In the top right of the photograph it is just possible to make out a small Christ pinned to a crucifix, like another insect to be examined. Across the thin neck of the old man are the words **BY DAVID FRANKLIN** in a much larger type than the title itself.

The Title Page

At the top of the page is the dedication, 'To my friend and editor, Stephen Glasgow, with gratitude.' Below it is written, in thick letters pressed heavily down on the page:

The damned book went to the printers before I could alter the dedication. Of course it's for you, Georgia. With all my love, David.

Around these sentences have been drawn dozens of blue roses, growing out of a thin line of soil marked in black ink. Below these doodles the author biography appears.

'David Franklin was born in Queensland in 1948. After reading English at the University of Sydney, he became a lecturer there, and published his first book of essays, *Australia: The Infantile Culture*, to great acclaim in 1978. Since then, he has written six novels, including the award-winning, *Harry's Joke* (filmed by Bruce Beresford in 1987), the *Newcastle* sequence, and a book of poems, *Sleep Woke Up*. He has been the recipient of many literary awards and fellowships. He is currently professor of English literature at the University of Newcastle.'

The biography then continues in blue pen, the first word tipped from the mouth of a daffodil. The handwriting is large and nervous and scrawly, like a child's on a wall.

> David Franklin recently married the very beautiful Georgia, who was born in Sydney in 1970, as Georgia Black. Her first story, 'What I Done in my Holidays', was received with great acclaim by her classmates in Year 3. She has been the recipient of only one prize, a gold star for correctly spelling the word 'antidisestablishmentarianism' at a school spelling bee. She studied English literature at Newcastle Uni for two years, before dropping out to marry her lecturer, David Franklin. She enjoys reading and writing, and doodling in books as she reads them, a habit that infuriates her new husband.

Then

> ~~Georgia Black~~
> Georgia Franklin
> G. Franklin
> Georgia Alice Franklin
> Georgia A. Franklin
> ~~Mrs David Franklin~~
> Georgia

Page 5

On this page, every 'o' has been carefully filled in with blue ink and transformed into a love heart. The first paragraph of the novel thus becomes:

CHAPTER ♥NE

He l♥♥ks up at the wires strung tight between the teleph♥ne p♥les, making the white sky seem like lined n♥tepaper, and the still silh♥uettes ♥f the cr♥ws arranged ♥n the lines a strange, f♥rg♥tten script.

Pages 22 to 23

Inserted between these pages is a Polaroid photograph of a man and woman holding hands. The couple stand, smiling, by the rail of a ship. The man (the same as on the front cover, if a little older) is wearing a creased white shirt and dark trousers, and his face is red with the sun. He looks uncomfortable, as if he would be happier in a black and white – or perhaps even sepia – photograph.

The woman has short dark hair, and smooth skin, except for fine wrinkles like cracks around her large dark eyes. The man is smiling his crooked smile, and the woman a shy one. She is pretty in her way, with a face that would look best framed by a veil, for first communion or a wedding.

Page 25

The margins of this page are surrounded by drawings of lips: some full and thick, others pursed in disapproval, some with a long tongue sticking out.

Pages 46 to 47

Red wine has been dribbled across the left page, and before it has dried the book has been closed over, giving a perfectly symmetrical stain on the right page. The pattern resembles a psychological test, and beside it has been written in a leaky red pen, giving the impression that the words are slurred: *A butterfly? Two angels? A man and woman copulating?*

Pages 64 to 65

Between these two pages is a small, neatly cut out article from *Australian Woman's Weekly*, entitled, 'How Happy is Your Marriage? Take Our Quiz!' The following options have been underlined with a black pen.

1. B. <u>Less than once a month</u>
2. <u>D. Missionary</u>
3. <u>D. Never</u>
4. <u>A. He doesn't</u>
5. <u>B. Rarely</u>

6. <u>D. He becomes angry and defensive.</u>

7. <u>A. I don't know.</u>

8. <u>A. Lack of intimacy.</u>

9. <u>C. Too much time apart.</u>

10. <u>D. Yes, I still love him.</u> To which has been added in red pen, *I think!*

Page 72

A short strand of spaghetti has fallen on this page, randomly connecting the words, 'man', 'loss' and 'she.'

Page 85

This page is spattered with green stains, from what may have been pea and ham soup.

Pages 98 to 99

Between these pages are several grains of rice, like fossilised full stops. Written on the left hand margin:

Number of times David hasn't been home for dinner in past three weeks. IIII IIII III

Page 122

On the right margin, beside a very long dialogue concerning

the philosophical differences of Heidegger and Spinoza, the word *Yawn* has been written and underlined four times with increasing certainty.

Pages 143 to 154

Attached by a paperclip to the dog-eared page 154 is a business card that reads:

Bradley Rockwell
Blue's Plumbing
No Job Too Small
TEL – 02 5856 4711

The words are printed onto the Australian flag. Handwritten on the back of the card is:

My personal number 0444344353 I will plug <u>any</u> holes
Brad.

Then, in Georgia's handwriting, *Yuck!*

Page 175

Highlighted in yellow are the words in the middle of the page, 'If she had no paper she would write notes on her forearms, her legs, her belly. Knowing this, he would seize

her before she went into the shower, and try to read her.'
The yellow continues to the margin, where a comment
has been written. *This seems familiar …*

Page 184

The sentence, 'The white sun in the sky was like a
cataract,' has been underlined. Beside it is written one
word: *STOLEN!!!!!*

Page 192

<u>'His clothes were ill-fitting and didn't suit him, and he
suddenly reminded her of a hasty understudy wearing the
lead actor's costume.'</u>

And this! My dissertation – he took it from my dissertation!

Pages 199 to 204

Every sentence on these pages is underlined. Several
words have been stained by drops of water.

Pages 205 to 210

These pages have been ripped out.

Page 211 to 212

The bottom half of the page remains, and the handwritten

words on the right margin of page 211, *Says it isn't plagiarism, but it is. If only he would admit it, maybe I could forgive him!*

Page 214

In black marker, running through the text in the middle of the page, are the words:

> *black erred lowly*
>
> *black world leery*
>
> *bared clerk lowly*
>
> *label clerk wordy*
>
> *wacky rebel droll*
>
> *Bradley Rockwell*

Page 220 to 221

In the cleavage between these two pages, a single, red pubic hair lies coiled like an ampersand.

Page 261

In the blank following 'THE END' of the novel the following has been written:

> ~~Dear David, why can you never say you are~~
>
> ~~Dear David, you won't take responsibility so why~~

~~David, I can't live a lie any longer~~

~~The only reason you don't fuck your books is~~

~~because you are afraid of paper cuts~~

~~You stole from me, so I let myself be stolen from~~

~~you~~

The Back Cover

There are two quotes on the otherwise plain back cover. The first, from the *Sydney Morning Herald*, reads:

> 'Astonishing. In the figure of unfaithful wife Irene Blackwood, Franklin has created a character to rank beside Emma Bovary and Anna Karenina.'

The final quote is from the *Australian Book Review*:

> 'Few men can write women as well as [David Franklin.] He reads the secrets of the female mind like an open book.'

Separating the Cream from the Milk

Laura Bovey

I was just nine when my grandmother died from Hodgkin's Disease. She survived her beloved husband by one year to the day. The farm – my grandparents having no sons to work it – was sold within the month. Unlike my older sisters, I didn't get to experience much of farm life. During the summer holidays they used to bus up to Bourke to help Grandad with the fencing and feeding, returning with ruddy faces and sinewy brown limbs.

For me, the farm was a romantic place where closets contained bags of juicy black plums and the cream was warm from the cow. Billy Black, the boy from the neighbouring farm, and I used to chase mice in the hay barn and tease the dairy cows, with their swollen, rubbery teats. Come evening, the soles of our bare feet would be black. Billy enchanted me with his dimples, porcupine hair and fearless spirit. When I was with him, I felt like the only person that mattered.

Fairfield seems a world away from those days. But I can walk to the shops and it's a twenty-minute commute to my job at Telstra. For my twenty-sixth I had a combined birthday and housewarming party. When Mum offered me Grandma's milk separator, I was overjoyed. In my mind I had visions of solid timber tables dusted with flour, buttery scones hot from the oven served with homemade strawberry preserve and fresh cream. I converted my sunroom – a long rectangular room off the kitchen – into an old-fashioned parlour, positioning the separator in pride-of-place under the windowsill. I scoured markets and jumble sales until I found an old timber tripod stool and metal milk pail to make the experience more authentic. The trio sat solemnly in my sunroom, waiting, for two-and-a-half years. In that time, the closest I came to the old-fashioned life was a batch of lemonade and cream scones. Which I burnt.

Mum died in the winter. After the funeral, I went home and sat at the milk separator, dappled sun filtering through the leaves of the big gum outside and caressing my skin. I ran my fingers over the bulbous supply can, the aluminium cool to the touch, the dimpled surface testimony to years of arduous work. Sitting there at the separator, I felt connected to my grandmother, my mother. Right then I realised that I am a link in a chain of strong women who knew what it was to work the land – I, too, have farmer's blood in my veins!

It was surprisingly easy to source a fresh-milk supplier.

My oldest sister, Keiren, took more convincing to come down and teach me to use the separator.

'Crazy Maizy,' she declared, rolling her eyes the way she used to when we were kids.

Crazy Maizy, that's what they used to call me. Rolling their eyes and waving a dismissive hand in the air. Nobody took me seriously.

'Buy milk at the shops like a normal person. Next we hear you'll be grinding your own wheat. Crazy Maizy.'

Grinding my own wheat? I decided not to attempt that one until I'd mastered the separator.

Despite her cynicism, Keiren started turning up every first Saturday of the month: Devonshire Tea Saturday. It became our ritual. Our tradition. Keiren would prepare the scones (I still haven't mastered that art) while I separated the cream from the milk, and we'd talk about Grandma and Grandad's farm, Mum's kitchen, the hilarious antics of Keiren's two boys. My non-existent romantic relationships. Life.

'Remember the Blacks? Billy was as crazy as you were. They're in town,' Keiren declared as she turned the dough out onto the floured bench.

'I thought Mr Black died last year?' My hands trembled as I poured a thin stream of milk into the supply can. Billy was in town? I hadn't seen him in what — twenty years? The way my heart was dancing around in my chest at the mention of his name was ridiculous.

'Yeah, he did. Mrs Black is moving into the retirement village here. Apparently she had a bad fall a month back and broke her hip. What would she be now? Eighty? That woman is tough as they come.'

What about Billy? 'Really?' I set the bucket down clumsily, sloshing milk onto the linoleum.

Keiren fell silent as she started kneading, pressing her knuckles into the sticky, pliable dough. I clenched my own hands, resisting the urge to knock my sister to the ground and knead the information I wanted out of her.

'And Billy?' I tried to sound casual. Clenching the wooden grasp in my right hand, I opened the faucet with my left before turning the iron handle.

'He's helping his mum settle in. Perhaps he didn't turn out so bad after all, eh?'

I looked up in mid-rotation to find Keiren watching me closely. My traitorous cheeks heated like the waiting oven. Keiren laughed.

'Unlike my little sis.' She disappeared from view and I heard her rummaging in the draw for the cutter. 'He was keen to come over and sample your cream.'

'You talked to him?' The first of the separated skinny milk gushed out the spout, splashing into the waiting pail loudly.

Keiren laughed again. 'Don't get too excited, Crazy Maizy. You might spill the cream. We'll need every drop with the extra mouth to feed.' She pushed the cutter firmly into the slab of dough, extracted a soft, milky round.

'What? Who?' I stopped turning, handle forgotten.

'Billy Black. I thought you wouldn't mind if I invited him over.' Keiren's back was to me as she loaded the trays ready for the oven.

Billy Black was coming here? Now? I could feel my body preparing for fight or flight, my mind swimming as if suspended in a pail of warm milk, my heart beating erratically, my shoulders knotting. Taking a few deep breaths, I deliberately started turning the handle again. This was ridiculous. For all I knew, Billy was now an overweight, balding prick of a man with a boring desk job. And a wife and children. Surely I would've heard if he'd married, though?

Keiren slid the trays into the oven, shut the door and set the timer. She wiped her hands on her apron as she looked out the window toward the street. 'Perfect timing. Here he is now.' She walked away to open the front door.

The first drops of cream spurted out of the cream spout and into the glass jar, spraying the sides like splattering fruit. I strained to hear Billy's voice – perhaps it would give me some indication to what sort of man he'd grown into. I tried to check my reflection in the side of the supply can, but it gave only shadowy blotches, the shine worn away years ago. Crazy Maizy was right; I was crazy! Rolling back my shoulders, I tried to focus on the task before me.

'You made it.' There was the sound of footsteps in the hall, the door closing. I cranked the handle double-time, my knuckles white on the smooth timber.

'Good to see you again, Keiren. It's been a long time.' His voice was deep and smooth. Unrecognisable from the one I remembered as a child.

All too soon they were standing in the entrance to the sunroom. I pretended to be carefully examining the regulating chamber.

Keiren cleared her throat. I looked up to find four eyes focused on me. And blushed. Billy was taller than Keiren and twice as broad. Tanned, muscled limbs protruded from a blue Nike tee-shirt and khaki cargo shorts. He grinned, the smile reflecting in his grey eyes. His blond hair was darker, cut short against his scalp.

'Maizy. You're wearing shoes,' he said.

Keiren stood there, tilting her head towards Billy and furiously making eyes at me.

'Uh, hey Billy,' I managed to crackle out.

'Actually, it's Will, now. I haven't been known as Billy since I was in primary school.'

I quickly busied myself with the handle. It spun uselessly.

Billy – Will – stepped forward into the sunroom. 'Here, I think you'll find you're out of milk.' He picked up the bucket of unseparated milk. 'Mind if I give you a hand?'

I shook my head mutely.

'I haven't used one of these things since …' He poured a stream of milk into the supply can. 'Since you used to come visit the farm.'

The oven buzzer erupted and I jumped. Keiren excused herself.

I returned to turning the handle in sturdy rotations. Will put the bucket down before moving to lean in the doorway. I could feel him watching me. Sweat began to trickle down the back of my neck.

'Hard work,' I said, making a show of wiping my forehead.

'Our grandparents were amazing people,' Will said.

A second lot of separated milk gushed out the spout and splashed into the pail. I involuntarily jumped again. My body was wound up, every nerve aware of him. Standing in the doorway, watching me.

'So Maizy, are you still crazy?' he asked, his voice low.

A tray clattered on the bench and Keiren cursed.

Cream ejaculated from the spout into the jar.

I moved my foot so fast it caught the side of pail and almost turned it over. I lunged for it, catching it just in time.

Will laughed. 'I take that as a yes.'

Just then Keiren called out from the kitchen 'Scones are ready, kids! Come get them while they're hot! And don't forget the cream, Crazy Maizy.'

Puppet Fears

Gina Boothroyd

1.

The man came home, knapsack scarred, buckles polished, straps holding fragment souvenirs. Egyptian dust, Turkish sand, Flanders mud, Australian grit. No one to meet him; no one expected. Hails and hoorahs saved for another's war.

He went along the platform to the glass display case and looked at neat number rows for his train departure. The Orion Line would take him home to his mother's house. *My mother needs her son*, he thought. *Her letters crinkled with tears. So many lost in the army post*, he thought. *A loving mother writes often.*

Home to bury horror in the backyard and let it grow, an unwieldy thing pruned down year after year.

Between a dark, serge shoulder and a canvas bag, he saw a glimpse of soft, water curls. A reminder of Adeline. *Adeline awaits my return*, he thought. *Does Adeline still live in the house three back from the grocery corner? Would be nice to pay a visit. Nice to hear neighbourhood stories. Nice to see Adeline again. Someone to make a strong pot.*

The station tearooms had displays of sweet afters. He asked for tea and a fresh cream bun. Changed his mind twice while waiting to pay.

'Just back, then?' asked the powdered lady with the starched cap pinned to her hair.

He nodded and thought about pumpkin scones.

'You missed the band yesterday. They had a band play for you boys. Gee, was I proud.'

The man smiled and handed the woman his money.

'Lost my Harold, I did, rest his soul.' She sighed, placing tea things together. 'Henry takes care of me now'days. Lucky, I s'pose. You going home to somebody, luv?'

The man nodded, grinned and walked away with his tray. Some time before his train. Teatime, then over to platform twelve. He sat at a table near two women and their children, drawn to the sweetness of voice.

'Sarah, let Mama wipe your face. Good girl.'

A fair child blinked at him over a handkerchief.

'Have a sip of Mama's tea. Here's some for your doll.'

The child held a miniature tin cup to the mouth of an exquisite, curly-haired doll. The doll sipped once before the child discarded the cup and dabbed at the painted mouth with a napkin.

The man looked down at his cream bun. Topped up his cup. Looked up; her blue-lights were blazing. Simple surrender; he smiled at the child. She smiled wide, bestowed cuddles on her doll. He loosened. Licked fresh cream from his bun.

'Dr Bennett is worried about Daniel. Says it's strange for a boy not to play.'

A vertical line creased the young mother's brow. She cupped the boy's chin in her hand, the way perplexed mothers do.

'Why don't you play with your little friends, Danny?'

A tilt of his head released her grip, and he stared at his hands, limp in his lap, legs swinging self-conscious scissors.

'He doesn't, you know. Just clings to my apron all day until Grandpa comes home.'

The man tried to brighten the little boy with his smile, but the child's gaze just sank onto his lap. The little girl seemed to have the answer.

'Mama, I want a cream bun for Danny. Mama, I want a …'

The mother held the palm of her hand up to the child, continued conversation with her friend. Disregarded, the little girl picked up the tin cup and tilted it to her doll's mouth. Soon she was scissor kicking in time with her little friend's swinging legs.

The man wiped cream from his nose tip and the blob shaped a curve on his finger. As he stared at it, the finger became a little man with a creamy, white beard. He wiggled it to life and made the finger talk. Turning to the girl, the cream-bearded man asked for her name.

'I'm Sarah,' she whispered. 'Who are you?'

'I'm Skipper Salty, *arhaar*. I live on a ship on the sea.' Then he wiggled and bobbed as if on the waves of the ocean. Sarah clapped her hands on her thighs and lifted her shoulders to her ears in suppressed delight.

'How big is your boat, Skipper Salty?' she asked.

'It be a ship, dear child, a ship, *arhaar*, and a beauty. Big enough to take you and your friend a-sailing.'

The finger turned quizzically from this side to that, trying to catch the little boy's eye.

His legs soon slowed, and the boy sneak-lifted his eyes.

'*Arhaar*, there be the boy who looks a fine sailing lad. How'd you like to join young Sarah here for a cruise?'

His eyes asked Sarah and she bobbed her head, encouraging. The little boy nodded, unsure. Sarah clapped both hands madly and bounced in her seat.

'His name is Daniel and he's my next door neighbour and we used to play sometimes, but he's sad now.' She looked at the finger as she spoke, addressing Skipper Salty.

'Well, we can't have sad little boys aboard the *Laughing Mermaid*.

Daniel's lips parted. Expectant eyes searched the man's face.

'That be the name of me ship. Do you like it?'

Daniel was still, but for questioning eyes.

'Yes, yes. Is she really a mermaid?' Sarah asked hopefully.

'That you'll have to wait and see,' teased the skipper.

Daniel's hand cupped his mouth in a whisper to Sarah, but the skipper didn't let it go by.

'What be your question, my hearty little lad?' The finger drew closer to hear.

'Go on, tell the skipper,' ventured Sarah. 'He'll know if it's true.'

Daniel looked out from under low eyebrows and spoke to the little bearded man.

'Mummy says the mermaids took Daddy when his ship fell over in the sea. And he can't come home 'cause he's happy sleeping now. And the mermaids make him stay.'

The man felt the cream turn to oil and slip down his finger.

'Your mummy be wise and she tells you the truth, but your daddy didn't choose it this way. You're a very good boy and your dad wants to be home, but he can't choose both home and the sea.'

The children blinked, waiting.

'I can't say why. Nobody knows. It just has to be that way.'

It was unfair to expect pure acceptance.

'Your daddy be with you whenever you need him, when your dreams bring him out of the ocean,' added the little bearded man.

Daniel smiled at the skipper.

'I knew he was home, but Mummy said don't say it.' Happily, he pulled his socks up to his knees.

Sarah said, 'Seeeeeee, the skipper knows things.' Then she leapt from the chair, pulling at Daniel for a game. 'I'm the skipper,' she sang. 'You're a mermaid.'

Sarah twirled and Daniel spun, perhaps like the dreams in his head.

'A time and a place,' scoffed Sarah's mother. With apologies to her friend, she called the little girl from the game.

'Sarah, come and sit down please,' she insisted, but Daniel's mother gripped her friend's arm.

'No, Doreen. Let them play this time. Daniel hasn't … not since …' Her eyes begged and beamed all at once.

The man wiped the oil from his finger onto his handkerchief and made his way thoughtfully across to platform twelve.

2.

The man remembered when his mother had rubbed bright pink on her cheeks. Now she slept often, worn out by the world that had funnelled itself through her pores. Penny novels filled her prostrate days. The sun made her shiver; the wind made her sweat. One consolation: her son with a pot of strong tea.

The kettle boiled. He poured the water into the old teapot and he stirred up the brew, watched the swirling brown leaves. Suppertime, not before nine, he remembered from habit, sitting down to watch the clock.

Tick. Tock. Five minutes to nine. *Tick. Tock.* Four minutes to go. *Hickory.* Three minute before. *Dickory Dock.* Two minutes, not long. Get the tray, get the cup, match a saucer, check the sugar, leave the milk. Two biscuits at the side to prompt the standard complaint.

'Two? Two biscuits? I'll never eat two.'

But they never returned to the tin.

At home now. Mother tucked up. A moment to think about things. Adeline gone. Married away. Better forget about Adeline. A soldier this morning, what now? A butcher? A miner? A drover? He tried to think of the work ahead of him but it was nicer to think of the fair, little girl and her sad, little friend. He sipped his strong cup of tea and smiled over that morning's play.

'Hello, Mr Finger,' wiggled his left, index finger.

'Hello to you, Miss Pointer,' waved the one on his right.

'What do we do with ourselves? We can't go back to The Store.'

'Why not, Miss Pointer? Why not?'

'Unbearable to think of going back. March forward always, you see?'

'I do, Miss P, that I do. But, what of it now? What to do all the long day?'

'And through the dark, dark nights, Mr F.'

'Yes, so dark, so true, Miss P.'

'We'll have to sleep on it.'

'Is it that easy, Miss P? Is that all?'

'Precisely what we will do.'

'Hmmm.'

'We dream, Mr F. We dream.'

The man slept deeply on his thin stuffed mattress and coils. The next day, his whole life woke up. He went to a haberdashery store, ducked amongst tall rolls of fabric and dexterous girls.

'The length, sir?' asked the matronly manager.

He looked down at the roll. Scratched his head.

'Perhaps enough for a dress, a skirt or a blouse?' she persisted, harried today.

He pointed to where she should cut. Bought six lengths in blue, green, yellow, black, red and brown.

Continuing along the main street, the man paused for a full six minutes before walking into The Store.

The third generation store owner stood behind the counter. 'Oh, it's you. Welcome back. If it's about your old job, no luck here, I'm afraid. Had to fill it when you took off. Saw the world, bet you did. Good of you to call in. Good-o, then. Drop by again. And if you ever need a pot of good paint …'

The man put a large jar of glue and some twine on the counter. Handed money to the store owner. He went to a store a few streets away to buy little pots of good paint.

Walking home, heavy hands, lighter step, he passed

the green park where he'd played, aged eight. Soon to go on, back to that time. Before wounding, before death stench, before gunfire barked at his life.

In the backyard he mulched up old papers with water and globs of thick glue. Squeezing and working his hands in the bucket, over an upturned basin he splattered the goo strips and sculptured a wide friendly face.

'I'm Puffy Piecrust. It's time for sweet cake with fluffed cream. Yum, yum.'

The face was laid on the grass to set in the sun. The smile poised, sun struck forever.

The man's hands worked themselves into withered wrinkles as they returned time and time again to the goo. That day bore Charlie Choo Choo, Wee Milly and the beautiful Baby Sue (whom he promised to find lovely curls), Tubby Drum, Mr Pot, Madame Silk and a wise cat he called Kitty Paw. All lay with faces steadily drying along a flat plank he found in the grass.

He squatted on haunches staring at the grey, gluey faces, seeing them coloured with life. For a long time he watched them, not trusting what would happen if he left them alone for a time. Every so often he looked towards the house to check for his mother's appearance. No, she would be happily absorbed with a thin, penny novel that she would hastily conceal under her pillow when he knocked at her door with the next tray meal, and sulkily complain of boredom and neglect. He lit a cigarette, blew smoke into soft breeze and returned to no-man's land. Eventually, with one gentle finger, he pushed at the goo; it felt firm, but not ready to paint. So, one by one, he moved the faces to the lean-to where they could safely spend the night.

At five past nine, he sat with the coloured fabrics and imagined bright garments and suits. Suddenly wishing he had bought softer colours for his wonderful Baby Sue, he noticed a doily and a length of cream damask on the sideboard under his mother's silver tea set. It would soon be scrounged to reappear proudly as a pinafore for his Baby Sue child. The night was short and busy as the man cut into the fabrics and plundered his mother's sewing basket, plucking buttons and ribbon thread treasures. He recalled the memory of long, rainy weeks playing with this bottomless basket while Mother sewed gowns. She would wear the gowns into the biting night when the gentlemen knocked at the door.

Stay back. Off to bed now. He's coming up the path. Out of sight now. Mother won't be long. The clown in the cupboard will keep you safe, and when you wake up, Mother will be here.

At daybreak, before his eyes opened, he thought of the paint pots and hurried to wash and to dress. On top of his knapsack, propped in the corner, was the pile of sewed clothes.

His mother, with her breakfast tray fastening her to the bed, would be occupied for the next hour or so. He lifted the lids of the paint pots slowly, like exhuming small sighs of life. Old knives made good stirrers, and a board from a crate a palette, where he mixed up a pink, fleshy tone. All the faces were flesh-washed with glossy, pink skin and set again on the plank to dry.

He repeated the process throughout the day. Adding lips and cheeks before morning tea, and eyebrows and nostrils up to lunch. The eyes with their clearly spoken detail took the rest of the day. He saved his precious Baby Sue for last, after Mother's suppertime.

By midnight his faces were impatient for life, and he promised they'd walk and talk soon.

Wednesday begot paper goo hands; Thursday, pillow torsos and limbs; Friday begot kitchen twine sinews; Saturday, crowned furry, felt hair, Baby Sue with cotton wool curls. Returning the puppets to the plank, he sat them all in a row. Puffy Piecrust, chubby and friendly. Charlie Choo Choo, an unstoppable dancer. Wee Milly, elusive, divine. Baby Sue, everyone's sugary sweetheart. Tubby Drum, boomingly big. Mr Pot, witty and wise. Madame Silk, exotic and proud. Kitty Paw, the contented feline voice of reason.

The man saw everything that he had made, and, behold, behold, behold, his new life as a puppeteer.

3.

The man went forward, encircled his past. Back to the green park he left at eight years of age. It was Sunday and children played on swings. Women, the mothers, and men, the fathers sat on blankets and benches dotted over moist grass. Dappled light distracted them from their role as parents and placed them in a world of lovers, connected by slow, warm air, carrying pollens and potent scents. The children, blind to their unsupervised freedom, followed the leader, chased the ball, hung upside-down, played patty-cake, whispered secrets, yelled at injustice and cried demands. They were glorious in the ways of being children.

The man scouted for a comfortable place in the shade. He placed his two sacks by a bench on the rim of the green, hearing hollow knocks as the contents complained. What a perfect day for debuts.

Kitty Paw was on top, no surprise to the bunch, and she sprung out to curl up on the bench slats. Charlie Choo Choo helped the others out of the sack, glad he wasn't sharing with Puffy Piecrust. He handed out Baby Sue. Wee Milly floated onto the grass. The second sack unravelled the rest of the group. Mr Pot apologised for an unchecked elbow placing pressure on the tummy of Tubby Drum. Thank goodness for Madame Silk, a mediator accustomed to discretion in such tight spots.

They sat in a line, expectant and happy and shy. The man in the middle whispered words to them, encouragement masking his nerves. Feeling his heart beat big in his chest, it was the life pump for the eight puppets.

A girl pointed from her place on the swings, and soon many more children saw the colourful bodies of paper and felt. The man turned to his puppets, asked for their help, and everyone responded in time.

'Hello.'

Careful. Controlled.

'Hello, children.'

'Come on, sit down here.'

Confident. Creative.

'We want to tell you a tale.'

'Not a tale, Tubby Drum. Stories, real stories.'

'What's our story today?'

'Shhh. Watch with your eyes and your heart and you'll see.'

The man sat in the middle of the bench and watched his puppets burrow into child souls. The tender, sewed clothes surrounded him now, reached out to crossed legs on the grass. Fuelled by the smiles and small peeps of delight, the man provoked puppetry bliss. The story progressed as promised and the children let laughter escape. Every organ, every limb, jiggled joy. Big breaths of excitement, a covering of eyes, a trick and a gasp and glee. The laws of the fantastic brought back to balance. Resolved with visionary thrills.

The parents looked up, peered through the insects and seed fluffs that masked the expanse.

'What are the children doing?'

'They are laughing.'

'At what? Where's the joy?'

'Inside our children. Can't you hear it?'

'I can. Incredible! What's the game?'

'It's him. That man. He has dolls all around him.'

'They're puppets. He's giving a show.'

'A puppet show! Marvellous!'

And the parents drew closer, curious to know joy in the world.

The man saw the women and men, standing and looking, walking his way. Invasion. Puppets leapt into sacks. Over his shoulders they clunked together and bounced from the park without protest. He was gone by the time the dazed parents reached the bench.

The children's re-telling was vivid confusion.

'Puffy Piecrust was naughty but Wee Milly saw him and Mr Pot complained. But when Tubby Drum found Madame Silk, Kitty Paw had to step in, because Baby

Sue loved to see Charlie Choo Choo dance, so, Wee Milly stuck stars on her face. Then we were singing and rhyming and … and …'

The parents wrapped their children away from sudden chills, not knowing what happened that day. And the man emptied his sacks, cleaned up his puppets and set them to rest in the lean-to.

Mother's tea was on time, as was her supper. The next day, a new package arrived. He held the string ties and rustled the brown paper.

It was the next penny novel, in time.

4.

The week ticked along through meal times and tea, with story thoughts noted between. The man smiled with each *tock* towards Sunday, when his body would glow warm and the puppets would awake from their slumber.

Diving into the sacks, forgetting complaints, the puppets knew how to behave. Time to grow hope at the edge of the Sunday green park.

'Here we are again. Would you like another story?' the puppets softly teased.

'Yes please, tell a story,' the children sung and squealed.

'Dear, dear, did we remember to bring our story today?'

'Please, ready now, please, please, please.'

The story began and laughter did spring from them,

and joy too. The stories were lessons in nonsense. Funny and shocking, absorbed by innocent brilliance. The man didn't know it, that love filled his stories. He only hoped for the smiles in return. It filled up his being and kept his soul buoyant, to drift through the meaningless week.

This pattern formed in his life. Every Sunday to the green park. Thrill children with puppets. Live on that joy through the week, marked by each brewed pot, until Sunday, to the green park again.

The man didn't notice the parents anymore. They stood at a distance, first enticed, then engaged, then enthralled. On the third Sunday, after the story was shown, Madame Silk whispered something to Charlie Choo Choo. He told Mr Pot, who thought the idea was a good one and suggested that Kitty Paw present it to the man.

'Put down a hat,' said the wise Kitty. 'A collection for us and for you.'

'I need new shoes,' prompted Baby Sue.

'And I'd like a small violin,' Tubby Drum boomed.

Wee Milly was silent and the man wondered at her thoughts. She was worried about being paid.

'We don't want to stop doing this for the joy, and money can do that, you know.'

'No fear of it,' helped Puffy Piecrust. 'We know why we want to come here. We are rich in everything else. The money will keep us in excellent shape and allow us to play more and more.'

As the oldest, he commanded respect, except when it came to table manners, and the group showed their hands in support of the idea.

Tubby Drum was elected to command the generosity of the parents in donating a coin to the show.

'We'll be back next week. Can't wait to see you. Goodbye now, and thank you. Goodbye.'

The man collected a sizable purse that day, and the next week, and then the next. His disbelief was set aside, as was the money, to live for his days in the park.

Eventually, it was Sunday. Eventually, It was a rainy Sunday. Not just rainy; stormy. Hail, lightening, screaming wind. The puppets chattered, their hollow limbs terrified of dangerous, soaking rain. Those storms never lasted long, but children don't go out in the rain, and parents don't take children to parks on wet days.

Eventually it was Sunday again. A rainy Sunday again. The man sat at the kitchen table. Listened to the pings on the tin roof with his head in his hands, waiting for nine o'clock, suppertime. The puppets huddled afraid in their sacks.

'Will he take us into the rain?'

'Of course not. He made us, he loves us, he'd never destroy us.'

'He loves the children more …'

They drew closer together, looked around in their sacks for warmth.

Finally, Mother got what she wanted. With a habitual complaint, she died. The penny novels had begun to build up on the bedside, a sure sign that something was nigh. No more regular meal times now. No more precisely timed tea. The penny novels arrived all the same. Unwrapped in a pile near the door. His life lost its clockwork routine and it rained on Mother's prepaid funeral day.

5.

That's when the man decided to buy a shop. A puppet shop of puppet times. It was Kitty Paw's idea, the one who most detested unpredictable weather, and the others rallied together, convinced it would save them all. The man was shown through a vacant shop in the High Street, accompanied by a bloke in pinstripes, and a barrage of false flattery.

'A fine young man, like yerself, won't do better in the heart of town,' said the bloke who had to sell. 'Noice and cosy fer impressin' the ladies too.' He winked over a glint and a nudge. 'You AIF? Thought so … So, whadda yer reckon?' he asked as he unfurled a flourish of hands toward the dunny door.

Mother's house, with the kitchen table, the lean-to, the backyard, Mother's room, the tin roof and the clock, was sold. The penny novels were stacked in the thunderbox. Handy. The two-storey terrace shop, with small living quarters upstairs and a patch of rear yard, was bought at a reasonable price.

With appropriate paints purchased from a shop a few streets away from The Store, the man painted a simple message on the glass door.

PUPPET TIMES

4 O'clock School Days
2 O'clock Saturdays

And Also At
10 O'clock Through Holidays

They all agreed to maintain the collection hat at the end of the puppet show, rather than ask for an entrance fee, the money never important at all. Now they were in business, together.

'Hello, children!'

'Hello, Tubby Drum!'

'Would you like a story?'

'Yes, please. A story! A story!' they chanted. 'A story!'

The man worked the puppets hard, and so success followed. Children came after school, bounced in on Saturdays, and arrived in waves through holiday breaks. And on the first anniversary of the shop's opening day, the man hinted at a surprise.

'What is the surprise?' wondered Wee Milly.

'Maybe a cake,' Puffy Piecrust licked lips.

'I think a holiday,' hoped Mr Pot.

'Or a new dress,' Baby Sue clapped her hands.

'There is no surprise,' doubted Madame Silk. 'We know his thoughts before he does.'

'I'd like us all to go to a show,' said Tubby Drum. 'Wouldn't you?'

Charlie Choo Choo had to agree.

'That would be nice, being in an audience for once. I'm tired some of the time.'

Kitty Paw waited for them to have their say.

'Let's not wish for anything. Let us see what comes.' And she licked her paws to show how easy it was to be a wise cat.

The man came down from his quarters upstairs, holding a limp, velvet sack. The puppets held the collective breath they never had breathed, and waited for the unveiling. From the sack the man pulled his surprise – a new puppet crafted from plaster-of-Paris. His features were terribly fine. Much finer than theirs. His fingers with smooth, indented nails. His lashes were genteelly curled. His hair looked real, but that couldn't be, and the flesh on his face appeared soft.

'His skin has small pores,' marvelled Wee Milly. 'And look in the depth of his eyes.'

They looked and they blinked at the new generation of puppet to join their ensemble.

'Hello,' he uttered, with deliberate distance. 'I will introduce myself by my stage name, since you will know me as a professional. I am Townsend Combe. How do you do?' And the new one bowed deep, to impress.

The man showed the fine one around the puppet stage and introduced the old players to him. Then they all rested for the 4 o'clock show; no one dozed, slightly dazed, a bit hurt.

Townsend Combe, keen to make his debut, warmed up his vocals and limbs.

'Oooooo, pretty,' cooed Baby Sue.

'Show off!' scoffed Mr Pot.

Wee Milly whispered into the ear of Madame Silk, 'Must he do that?'

'Obviously, he must, my dear. The question is, why?'

'Bravo, Combe,' declared Tubby Drum, too keenly.

'Did I hear the kettle whistle, just now?' enquired Puffy Piecrust. 'It's just that, the day seems like any other … but somehow … different.'

Charlie Choo Choo was tapping along to Combe's strange manoeuvres. 'He's out of time,' he said, satisfied.

Kitty Paw curled up like an unborn babe. 'We are all out of time today.'

At a quarter to four the man helped Combe dress in a tailored, white linen suit.

Ready in the wings, the routine had changed, and the puppets clunked heads, over fussed.

'Hello, children.'

'Hello, Tubby Drum.'

'I said … HELLO, CHILDREN.'

'HELLO, TUBBY DRUM!'

At least this part on the show was old ground.

'Guess what this day is. It's our BIRTHDAY!'

'Hooray!'

'And guess who is coming today?'

'Who? Is it Puffy Piecrust, Baby Sue, Charlie Choo Choo, Wee Milly, Mr Pot, Madame Silk and Kitty Paw?'

'Yes! And who else?'

'You! Tubby Drum!'

'And who else?'

The children thought hard, expecting a trick, and declared, 'There is no one else.'

'There is now. Let me introduce to you the latest recruit for this time of puppets – the noble, the impressive, the only, TOWNSEND COMBE.'

'Hooray!' cheered the children.

So much was their trust of their old paper maché friend.

The newcomer glided onto the stage. Silence frosted the fantasy. Townsend Combe paused, sensing the awe.

'Goooooood. Such good, quiet children,' with softness he spoke. 'Let me tell you a secret.' The children drew closer, felt the command of the new, smooth operator. He noticed a thread lying loose on his breast and delayed to remove it with a distasteful flick to the floor. Then, without shifting tone, he reported his message, as cool as he'd been all the day.

'Life is brief and beautiful. There is too much to do and to see to be cooped up indoors watching silly handmade puppets full of nonsense, pretending that play is important.'

An urgency infiltrated his inflexion.

'Time is all you have … and you don't have that forever. So play in the creek, chase after your frogs and fish, but know that it all comes to nothing. Better to get on with the business of living life as it's going to be.'

Combe looked over the heads of the crowd silhouette, awaiting any response. Some looked to their friends, questioned with eyes, shrugged and puzzled and wondered.

'A little about myself,' continued Townsend Combe.

The puppets weren't given a chance to counteract the disagreeable delivery and shamed themselves into their sacks. The man never looked over their way. Who wants to see hurt of that kind? Alone on the stage the puppet superior inflated his chest like a cock. And the man felt the pride of having found a new friend who deems you worth having around. He sat like a child, waiting for Townsend

Combe's amazing one-man puppet show. Nothing moved, no one spoke. Townsend appeared to freeze.

'You are supposed to help me,' hissed Combe through the side of his mouth. The man's head shook – a sign that he couldn't. It was up to the new puppet breed.

'So now, dear, *good* children,' coaxed Combe to the young ones, 'our puppet show cannot go on. But tomorrow there will be more surprises, *I promise.*'

Satchels and piles of books wrapped up with leather straps were located and hauled over small shoulders, more burdened than when they arrived. Eyes looked down, feet shuffled, nothing was said. Left, right, left, right, out and home they marched.

One little boy paused in the doorframe, raised on tippy-toes dodging schoolmates to see the big sacks to the side of the stage.

'Goodbye, Wee Milly,' he whispered to his favourite.

He ran home too fast to see tears. The man watched the boy through the shop pane. Thought of dead fathers and mermaid confusion.

6.

Up early the next day, the man fixed a big, cooked breakfast, wishing he could eat it on a terrace in the sun. The fine Townsend Combe was propped at the table, claiming to have had a hideous night. The linen suit still hung elegantly and his slicked hair was unruffled, but a hideous night was a fashionable thing with which to avoid conversation.

The man had to travel the distance across town, the same secret journey of yesterday. Scooping on shoes as he plunged down the stairs, eyes avoiding the stage and the sacks.

The train to the city and the light rail to *The Importers' Emporium*, where more fine puppets hung from the shelves. Over the door was a painted promise – *Bringing the Treasures of the Globe to All Corners of the Earth*. It was like stepping into the world in miniature.

'If it fits on a ship, it will be in my store,' promised the importer as the man waded through to the back.

There they were, Townsend Combe's friends – Monty Umbridge and Felicity Lipp. He needed their finery in the new show; Townsend deserved nothing less. The collection in the hat was devised as a means for improvement. What better way than to spend earnings on a more refined class of entertainer? Secure in their velvet sack, he was bringing them to their new home.

Taking the light rail back to the city, a crowd had built up at the central station.

'Come, come people. I'll ask you to delay your journey. Been an accident down the line, so please delay your journey,' repeated the station master. 'I don't know the details, but no sense in making the chaos worse down the line now, is there?'

Some chose to walk. The man looked at his watch. Still early, he knew what to do. The train station tearooms had excellent cream buns, and he hadn't sampled one in a long time.

'Out for the day, then?' asked the powdered lady, who looked less seriously starched than last time.

The man smiled at her kindness and pointed to the cream bun under the glass display case.

'They're your favourite, aren't they? Yes, I remember you. You're the man what played with them children in 'ere, oooh, long time ago now.' She winked and felt clever. 'I never forget a face.'

He was startled at the loss of anonymity. Sat a long way from the counter, poured tea. Undetected, the man watched her wipe over a bench top and finally disappear into the back as she peeled off her starched, puffy cap and retrieved a cigarette. His tea went down more easily with her departure, and he bit heartily into the bun. As he wiped the cream from his nose, he heard the little girl Sarah and the sad boy Daniel speaking in secrets from the sack on the opposite chair.

'Yes, he does, Daniel. He still loves us. Only he forgot what we love about him.'

The boy whispered something the man didn't hear, but Sarah spoke clearly again.

'No, he's not with the mermaids, but he once *nearly* was. It was close, and he was late home. He saw lots of bad, bad things. *Bad* things that he doesn't even remember anymore. They got hidden under the children's laughter and that was good for a while, but he wanted to show them the bestest time yet, so they wouldn't ever go away. He had to find someone better than him. They deserve it, after all.'

The man reached into the sack and pulled out Felicity Lipp.

Disappointed, he searched for Daniel but found Monty Umbridge. Slumping, the man chewed down his bun. With his teacup drained, he left the tearoom, left the sack, left the impostors there too.

It was a quarter to four when the man walked into his shop, but he didn't hurry the puppets to readiness. He didn't take Townsend Combe through the warm-ups. Didn't even look at the dead sacks by the side of the stage. The man sat in the shop window and waited. The school bell had long tolled, and still he waited.

He waited for no one, for he knew there was no one to come.

Townsend Combe was found dumped on a pile of old furniture. He was lucky. No food scraps, or mud, or rain had tarnished his plaster complexion. His white, linen suit was touched with grey dust, though far from being too offensive. The little ragged girl thought she had uncovered a treasure at first and ran home with her spectacular find, but within a short time, Townsend Combe was on the scrap heap again; not so lucky this time. An eggy, vinegar-pungency attached like a monogram.

The man retreated from the window of his shop into the living quarters upstairs. Into the life he lost on fields – fields now sprouting grass and dainty flowers once more. He stayed with the souls who sank their lives in mud. Mud pies. Dirty knees. The shop grew darker as he stopped opening drapes to the day. One day he took planks from the patch of backyard and nailed them over the shop's front window and door. No one wanted in. No one wanted out.

He kept an oil lamp next to the mantle clock and introduced a vigil for his dead mother. Breakfast, tea, luncheon, tea, dinner with tea, supper. A transition began – he economised his needs; he over-economised his needs; he ignored his own needs.

An empty shell waiting to wither.

A cold house for a child.

The routine etched no impact on the outside world. Children forgot about puppets and turned to bicycles and dollhouses and things they found in the creek. The new game was an old game. Children played soldier. Children played nurse. Children won wars.

'Die, I tell you. It's your turn to die.'

And the outside world etched no impact on the man. Darkness constantly cloaking, dust mites silently choking, the puppets in their sacks by the stage.

[58]

Hot Water Bottle

Belinda Campbell

Mum keeps pouring the water too fast, so it hits the rim and spills out the lip and burns her hands. Then she says *Shit* and puts the lid on before it's even half full. I tell her she has to squeeze the air out of it first, like Mrs Brindle does when we're allowed to take our hot water bottles to school, but Mum says she doesn't have time for that, and when I tell her I can do it, she says, *You can't because you might burn yourself.* So I ask her why it's okay for her to get burnt but not okay for me, but I can tell it's a silly question because her lips scrunch up tight like a cat's bum.

I know Mark hasn't noticed her lips because he tells her he's not going, and then he crosses his arms and sits on the couch, and that makes her lips get even tighter. Mum hands me the water bottles and then she pinches Mark's ear and drags him out. And even though I let him have the blue one, which is his favourite, he slams the car door anyway.

It's cold and at least I've got a hot water bottle, but it only keeps my lap warm so I ask Mum to turn on the heater but she says it's broken. Mark says he can see the orange light on the dashboard and *That's a warning.* And then he says we're going to run out of petrol and get stuck and die and Mum says, *Don't be such a drama queen*, which I don't understand because he's a boy and that means he should be a king. So I ask why but nobody hears me.

Then Mum puts the radio on and I can tell she likes the music because she's rolling her head around like they do in the videos and tapping on the wheel, but then she starts to cry and Mark says the bad f-word, then turns it off. Mum tells him she'll wash his mouth out with soap if he's not careful, but she doesn't put the music back on.

She parks across the road from Uncle Jim's house and, even though I know that he's not really an uncle, I call him that anyway because Mum says, *He may as well be one*. Mark doesn't call him anything anymore or even talk or look at him and I think that's why Uncle Jim doesn't come out and give us Freddo Frogs anymore.

It's dark because we're not under a street lamp and I ask Mum if we can go under a street lamp instead, but she just tells me to cuddle my water bottle and *There's a blanket behind the backseat* if we need it. She wipes the leaky black from under her eyes and reaches over Mark to get her lipstick out of the glove box. Then she locks the doors and I know she's taken the keys with her because she shakes them in her hand when she walks away.

I watch her knock on Uncle Jim's door, and just before it opens she turns around and mouths, *Don't go anywhere*, so I nod and then we pretend we're stranded on an island so we can't go anywhere anyway. And Mark uses the cigarette lighter as a telescope and even though I know he's lying when he says there are sharks in the water I pull my toes up from the car floor anyway.

But then the windows start to fog up and Mark tells me it's because I'm breathing too much, and if I keep on breathing there won't be any air left for later. So I try and hold my breath like I'm under water but it hurts my chest and it's hard because I know it's air that I need, and there's plenty outside, and all I have to do is get to it. So I tell him I'll just roll down the window instead, but he says, *You can't because you need the keys for that*. And now I wish that Mum hadn't taken the keys with her, and I wish that I could go in to Uncle Jim's house and find her and maybe he'd give me a Freddo Frog. But I can't because she said don't go anywhere and, anyway, there are sharks in the water.

Mark's telescope isn't working anymore and it isn't very much fun being stuck on an island, so we pretend we're on a ship instead, sailing away from the island, and I shake my hot water bottle because Mum didn't squeeze the air out of it so it sounds like waves hitting our ship. At first we're both pirates, but then Mark says that he's a pirate because he's a boy and I'm a prisoner because I'm a girl and now his telescope is a sword and I don't want to be a girl anymore. So I cross my arms and ignore him like Mum says I should when I want him to stop. But it doesn't work and he doesn't stop and he keeps on stabbing me and I wish that Mum were here because she would know how to make a pirate stop. I know I shouldn't cry but I can't help it anyway and then he calls me a cry-baby so I call him a drama queen. And then he says *Fine* and tells me *No more games* and sits and stares at the fogged up windscreen instead.

I can't see out my window anymore and it's dark when you're not under a street lamp so I cuddle my hot water bottle like Mum said I should but it doesn't make it any easier to see. I ask Mark if he wants the blanket but he isn't talking to me anymore, so I hand it to him anyway and pretend that I'm on a ship again. Then I draw a big round sun and a beach and a palm tree in the fog on my window and pretend that it's the island I'm sailing away from. And the wet comes off and drips down my finger.

When I close one eye and look out through the lines I've drawn I can see Uncle Jim's house, so I stare through the trunk of my palm tree and then I can see Mum pulling the door shut and stopping on the path and putting her shoes back on. And I wave at her when she looks up because I want to warn her about the sharks in the water but she must not be able to see me behind the foggy glass because she doesn't wave back.

I don't know how, but she makes it back to the ship alive, and then she gets in and uses her bare hands to wipe the windscreen, and I think she's brave for what she's done. And then I think she must be cold and Mark should offer her the blanket but he doesn't. And he doesn't even look at her, and I think that I would offer her a blanket if I had one.

Then she starts the car and I wish that I was sitting next to her instead of Mark because she doesn't know that boys are pirates and girls are prisoners, and anyway, I don't like how he gets to sit in the front seat just because he's older and I'm littler, and how that means he also gets to say bad words to her, which he does now and gets smacked for, and I tell her he's wrong but it's only when you're in the backseat that nobody can hear you.

Mum steers us around and takes us away and back the way we came and I wipe the sun and the beach and the palm tree from my window with my bare hands and wave goodbye to the sharks. We stop for petrol and Mark gets to pump because he asked nicely and Mum keeps saying sorry because his face is red. She gives him extra money for Freddo Frogs, and now it doesn't even matter anymore that the heater isn't working and my hot water bottle has gone cold.

Short Story Competition

Competitions are hard work. Not so much for us, although we have lots of reading to do, but for you, as authors. It takes a lot of courage to put your story not only out there, but to sit it alongside competitors who are trying to oust you. Because that's what happens in a competition. In the end, only a handful win and/or place.

Judgement in itself is subjective. For the 2013 *[untitled] Short Story Competition*, we tried something a little different. The competition was judged by a panel comprising (editor) Beau Hillier, (assistant editors) Daniel Kovacevic, Jodie Garth, Helen Krionas, and Danielle Gori, (publisher) Blaise van Hecke, and myself (chief editor). We voted, we discussed, we thrashed it out to find a consensus because, as readers, we all have different tastes.

Many stories are borderline equal but are unfortunately squeezed out through the selection process. In competitions like these, when there are numerous entries – and we had more entries than our previous two competitions – the decision on whether a story progresses or is cut can almost seem to be determined on a whim.

It's not, but the smallest query – e.g. an implausible character action, an undeveloped plot point, one moment of inconsistent pacing – can see one story fall by a wayside whilst another progresses through to the next round of judging.

This is why revision is always so important in writing, to iron out any problems. Also seek the opinions of other readers – people who'll give you constructive feedback, (as opposed to family or friends, who might tell you what you want to hear, may criticize you because they don't understand your aspiration to write, or who are simply evil).

It does show in reading when those details have been attended, and it's always a pleasure to be able to read a story, and to forget that you're actually meant to be judging it. This is what we want (and is *[untitled]*'s mandate): to read stories we can lose ourselves in.

Here now are the five winners of the *2013 [untitled] Short Story Competition* – and please be aware that these mini-assessments have been written with a view towards avoiding spoilers.

Highly Commended

Niall's Edge – Suzannah Marshall Macbeth

There is something haunting – a sense of imminent doom – interlaced throughout the writing here in a story about relationships and coming to terms with moving on and accepting inevitability. Also, great use of metaphor to parallel the fortunes of the relationship.

Highly Commended

Rollerbaby – Venetia Di Pierro

There's a beautiful lyricism about this voice in the story about adolescent idolisation and rebelliousness. Whilst it would almost seem to stand as a character study, the way the prose reflects on the narrator presents a broader picture – one character mirrors the other. You could almost imagine this as the theme for a young adult drama (as in a movie), akin to the stuff written by S.E. Hinton (*The Outsiders, Rumble Fish*).

Third Place

She's All Broken – Peter Hill

A compelling look at not only the difficulties of the disabled in everyday society, but also our perceptions of them. It's interesting how intelligence is correlated with language and communication, and the frustration that anybody who finds difficulty in those regards would experience. Here, the author includes a MacGuffin around which the story unfolds.

Second Place

The Human Child – Adrienne Tam

Adrienne came second in last year's competition with a great little horror story called *The Worry Man*, and she's backed it up with this story which is subtler in its approach and vacillates between horror and psychological thriller, while lamenting the protagonist's familial issues and reconciling that difficulty many of us face in going home, especially when confronted with disapproving or disappointed parent(s).

First Place

Regatta – Luke Thomas

There is a wonderful cerebral quality about *Regatta*, as the protagonist, Tom, deals with his growing estrangement from his wife whilst they are holidaying in Africa. Throughout, the story explores themes such as love, loss, union, and attraction, balancing them precariously whilst handing piecemeal information as to how this couple have become this way, while infusing in Tom a yearning for things to be the way they were – that sense many of us experience when confronted with trauma and wanting to go back to a better time.

And just a note before we go onto the stories, these stories have *not* been edited. You are reading them as they were judged. The very most we have done is a light copyedit to clean up punctuation.

Niall's Edge

Suzannah Marshall Macbeth

Niall comes out of the water and up the beach to the porch at the back of the house. The sea behind him is starting to gather height as the land breeze strengthens. *Bugger that*, he thinks. He doesn't like the way the waves on this break stand up beautifully in an offshore breeze, then dump you violently if you screw it up, straight down onto the pebbly bottom with only a few feet of water over it. He turns and watches as the water is sucked away to meet the next wave, which gains steadily in height, curving at the top, and then breaks and plunges in towards him.

He goes to step up onto the porch and stubs his toe on a raised plank. 'Shit.' A sliver of wood sticks under his toenail and he hesitates for a moment, board under one arm, knowing he'll topple over if he tries to pull it out with his other hand. He limps across the porch and leans his board against the wall. He bends down and plucks the splinter out from under his toenail. It leaves a little bead of blood and he pitches the splinter grumpily into the sand. There is sand spilling out from under the raised plank. On both sides of the porch the sand is building up, inundating the hardy dune bushes.

He peels off his wetsuit, looking out onto the bay. He heaves a sigh watching the waves picking up and feeling the change of the weather on his skin, the mellowing of summer air at the end of the season. He turns away to go inside. The back door is, as usual, jammed, and he has to wrench it violently to get it to open. He goes inside and lifts it back into place behind him.

He turns around and Sharna is standing in the doorway to the kitchen, leaning on the doorframe.

'What?' he says.

'The door,' she says.

'What about it? It's been like that for ages.'

'That's the point,' she says. 'The house isn't going to straighten out suddenly, you know.'

She turns and walks away from him down the hall. Her hair is in a plait down her back. He wants to walk after her and put his hands on her waist, invisible as it is beneath her baggy red jumper. But he doesn't, because these days she shrugs him off, looking at him as though there's something she doesn't understand. She used to surf with him; now she walks around the headland to the next bay and surfs there.

Niall used to like the drive along the coast road, winding along the wild edge of the continent with no hint of a town ahead and then all of a sudden curving around the big headland, and seeing the town before him. From that vantage point, the ocean occupies the horizon except for a small wedge of land where the town settles precariously, the harbour tucked away under the headland. The buildings are crammed onto the flat along the bay and the hills, thick with bush, rise suddenly behind the last row of houses.

The main road of the town is quiet these days, and in the shadows under the deep verandas most of the shopfront windows are empty. A little further on there's a row of old weatherboard houses, built in the days before anyone worried about planning permits. The one opposite the post office has a loose sheet of tin on the roof that flaps noisily whenever the wind gets too much south in it. Niall can hear it from his place at the other end of the strip of houses. It's not really his place, since it belongs to Sharna's grandparents, but he thinks of it as his own.

He's alone in the house tonight with the wind blowing steadily from the south. Sharna's been gone since Monday. She's not here to tilt her head when the tin starts banging and comment on the shift in the wind. He's glad of this, because she always seems on edge when the wind is in the south. But, as is usual by this stage of the week, Niall has started to miss her more than is comfortable, and the nights without her are long. He is fine in the first few days after she leaves, but as the days pass the house seems to get smaller and smaller, and the ocean bigger and closer every day. Yet it is still she who wants to leave this house, even though he is the one who is here alone most of the time, feeling the heavy mass of the ocean outside the back door.

Niall loves the ocean, loves it in the same way that he remembers loving the backyard of the house in Bentley when he was a kid. It scares him nonetheless. Some days it picks him up and throws him much too far for comfort. He comes ashore shaken, knowing he's been brushed by forces he can't comprehend. Sharna doesn't surf there anymore. She says the break is dangerous now, that it's changed over the years. He stubbornly clings to it, holding onto this dream of having a surf break right outside the back door.

All the same, he's not sure that he could spend days on end at sea on a fishing boat, like Sharna does. He likes knowing that the land is close by if he needs it.

He heads up to the pub for dinner. The publican nods at him but doesn't say hello. Niall is used to this: he knows he should start saying g'day first, but he always feels a bit fake. He's not from here and they know he's not from here, so what's the point in pretending? He orders a parma and salad and sits at a table by the window.

Wendy comes in the door at that moment, pushing her hair back with one hand. She spots him and crosses the room.

'Hey!' she says, smiling brightly as usual. Her face is pink from the wind and her lips are pale in contrast. She still has her green Department of Environment and Conservation shirt on. He likes the little logo with the leaves that look like waves. It's massive on her, of course. Seems the department hasn't gotten around to making shirts small enough for Wendy.

'Hey, Wendy, what's going on?'

'Not much,' she says. 'The boys are out having a smoke.'

'Grab a seat,' Niall says. 'I'll get you a beer.'

'Just a middie, thanks.'

When he comes back she is reading the newspaper. He's never quite sure where she manages to find a newspaper in this pub, but she always does. She has her back to the telly, on which some greyhounds are racing 'round an obscure track in NSW. She looks up as he comes over.

'So, Niall, how's the house doing?'

'It's all right,' he says. 'Bit lonely without Sharna, of course.'

'That's not what I meant. You two going to get another place soon? Before the winter?'

He looks at her. 'Sharna been speaking to you?'

'No,' Wendy says, surprised, 'but you'll have to get somewhere soon, right? You know what last winter was like. This coastline is changing all the time.'

Niall shrugs. 'We'll see what happens.'

She raises her eyebrows but doesn't push the point. 'So … what else?'

She's trying to draw him out, trying to get him to say more about himself. She's been trying this ever since he got here and it's been a while now. At least when he first moved to town he had the usual answers to give – he told her about work, where he'd come from, blah, blah. It's as though she thinks that he has more to offer, and these days, he's sure that he doesn't. His job has long since evaporated and she's heard all he had to say about Perth. There's nothing else. Surf, empty house, Sharna gone for the week … that about covers it.

As he runs through these things in his head, he knows that his life does sound empty. But it doesn't feel empty. Every day is full of the ocean, the massive ocean and the sand that sleeks its way inland, a little further each windy night. Every day is full of Sharna, and her absence and her presence. When she's home, the house is filled by her silences, until she snaps at him and he retreats, confused, wanting to make her happy like in the old days, but unable to shake her from her persistent argument that they must leave. And when she's away, her presence persists in every room of the house; a reminder to him that they cannot leave this place, because then he will have nothing left of her to hold onto while she is out there on the heaving, sighing ocean.

Saturday morning is calm and warm, the water stretching glassily away from the shoreline to the horizon. Niall sits on the edge of the back porch with a cuppa, his feet in the soft dry sand above the high watermark, watching the tide come in. In spite of the stillness, it progresses steadily. He is always surprised by the inexorable stealth of a flood tide.

There's no swell, so he goes inside after a while to make breakfast. By the time he's eaten and cleaned up, it's nearly midday and he goes back onto the porch to watch for Sharna's boat, *Blue Eyes*. The beach is deserted and towards town he can see the dilapidated back porches of the other houses lined up neatly, each one pushing its way onto the beach or holding its ground, depending which way you look at it. Niall remembers this town as it was when he used to pass through for work. It was yet another humming surf town of the southwest, and here, unusually, the locals clung fiercely to their beachside real estate in the face of the tourist incursion. But then, slowly, the ocean changed from Australia's playground into something to be avoided. It didn't take much: just a change in the way the currents worked along the coast, catching people by surprise, drowning a few here and there, scaring the others off. Freak waves and the winter erosion of coastal dunes began to make beachside living a little less palatable, as well as the dangers of summer cyclones that seemed to progress further south every year. By the time Niall moved to the town to live with Sharna, less than half of the beachside houses were occupied. The others were abandoned as the land and the buildings on them became suddenly worthless. He remembers Sharna telling him that she intended to live here as long as she could. At the time, people expected that the shire council would eventually condemn the houses and demolish them, and back then it had been neither here nor there to Niall whether or not they stayed in this house.

It matters now, though, as he watches for Sharna from the porch. The pressed-tin roof shadows the sun, which has already moved north and no longer has the white strength of midsummer, but is powerful all the same. The water is smooth and sparkling in the light and all around him there is stillness. It's a little humid, a little oppressive, and Niall thinks that maybe these will be the last hot days before winter.

After a while *Blue Eyes* comes into view around the headland, and Niall picks himself up off the scratchy wood of the porch. The lethargy of the morning is abruptly gone, and he wastes no time now, going inside for a clean shirt and then back out onto the porch. He steps onto the sand and walks down to the water's edge before turning towards the harbour, his feet in the edge of the sea.

At the end of the beach he jumps up onto the rocky sea wall and walks along to the jetty. *Blue Eyes* is just through the heads now, and he stops by her berth and waits. Johnny, the young bloke who helps on the boat, is at the bow with the boat hook, and when the boat swings into the pen he reaches down for the mooring lines that drift in the water. Sharna waves at Niall from the wheelhouse, and he smiles, waving back.

This is a regular thing, Niall waiting on the jetty as Sharna brings the fishing boat into the pen, her two crew working the lines while she's at the wheel. He is always glad to see her; glad to know she's back within reach. It took him a while in the early days to understand why he felt so good when *Blue Eyes* came into view around the headland. It was not just about love. Eventually he had to admit to himself that he felt relief, and that each time she was gone he felt afraid.

In the afternoon, when the boat is cleaned up and the catch offloaded, Niall and Sharna walk back along the beach together. 'How was it?' Niall asks, seeking the story that she always keeps hidden from him until this part of the routine.

She shakes her head slowly. 'Not good. We didn't have much luck at all. You saw how little we brought back. Would've stayed out longer but Johnny's sister's wedding is tomorrow.' She pauses, looking over at Niall, and smiles. 'But hey, it'll be okay. And the forecast is shit for the next week, so we won't be going back out for a few days.'

Her smile does not last long, and Niall, watching her, sees her look away from him. Her steps slow as though she has run out of energy. Her happiness at seeing him seems to disappear faster every time she returns. By the time they turn away from the shoreline and walk up the beach to the house, it is as though a barrier has fallen into place between them. She goes ahead of him to the back door, pulls it open, and heads down the hallway, leaving Niall standing there at the open door to watch her walk away.

A few nights later he is woken by rain, heavy on the tin roof, and a moment later there's the sound of thunder cracking outside. The bed is empty beside him and he's instantly tense, so he gets up quickly and walks into the hallway.

Sharna is standing at the back door, facing the ocean, her shape indistinct in the darkness. A cold wind is coming through the open door. 'Whatchya doing?' he says.

She doesn't answer, and so he walks down the hallway to her. She moves aside so that he can stand next to her.

The rain is louder now. It's pouring down past the end of the porch onto the sand and the foam of the waves. And, just then, a particularly big wave shoots right up and onto the edge of the porch. 'Shit!' He pulls Sharna back out of the doorway and slams the door, but it bounces and she turns away from him and walks away down the hall.

'WHAT?' he yells, moving after her.

She spins around abruptly. 'Now do you fucking believe me? The house is going to fall into the ocean!'

He stops, frozen. 'No!'

He turns abruptly to go out onto the porch, as he always does when they fight, but he can't. The water is right there, the rain is overflowing from the gutters, and the ocean is pounding at the doorstep. There isn't anywhere to go.

He turns back. Sharna has opened the front door now at the other end of the hallway and the wind tears straight through the house. He tries again to shut the back door but he can't against the force of the wind funnelling through. He yells at her, but she just stands there with the door open, looking at him. Then she lets it go and it slams shut. With the pressure off the back door, Niall lifts it into place in the architrave and suddenly it seems very quiet in the house.

There is still the rain on the roof and the wind outside but he can hear his blood pounding in his head. It's the sound of the ocean, the sound of a conch shell. He sees Sharna standing there, still looking at him, and the beautiful curve of her face is illuminated by the light from the bedroom. He feels abruptly that she is the only thing left. He can hear the slow drip-drip beginning in the kitchen where the roof leaks. The rain is still pouring down and he can hear the waves pounding outside. But Sharna – she is perfect, looking at him, and he takes an awkward step towards her.

In the morning the storm is gone and the sea is calmer but the air is cold: it's the cold of winter setting in. Standing in the doorway with the door hanging crookedly on its hinges, Niall realises suddenly that there is no sand to step easily onto at the end of the porch. He crosses to the edge, and has to jump down five feet onto sand that is hard and compacted from last night's waves. He sees that the stumps under the porch are exposed. The sand that has been building up under the house for months has disappeared and one of the stumps is loose, its foundations washed from under it.

He goes back inside and finds Sharna on the computer with the rental websites open. 'It's time to go,' she says.

'Go where?' he says.

'Inland. Out of town, maybe. But you have to get a job. No more free rent when we leave this place.'

'We don't have to go just yet,' he says.

'No?' she says. 'After last night? When do we go?'

'The house is still standing. It's not going anywhere this winter. We could move the stuff from the back rooms into the front rooms, you know, consolidate a bit.'

She shakes her head. 'What happens when the place really does fall into the sea? I've got to start thinking about what's next, Niall. I don't want to be here when the stumps get ripped out from under us.'

He turns away. *No, no, I want to stay*, he thinks. *It could be five years. We could have five years left. I want to stay.*

Later that morning there is a knock at the front door, and Wendy calls hello. Not waiting for an answer, she comes through to the kitchen.

'Niall, how's it going? That was some storm, hey?'

'Yeah,' he says. 'What's up?'

'We're going to look at the old Jackson place on the hill. They're looking for tenants. Hasn't Sharna said anything?'

Sharna comes in at that moment. 'Hey, Wendy.' She turns to Niall. 'Wendy and I are off to look at a place to rent. You can come if you want.' She pauses. 'Or you can stay.'

Niall doesn't know what to say. Sharna is looking at him. Wendy is still, waiting. After a moment he turns away and looks out of the window above the kitchen sink.

'Come on, man,' Wendy says softly.

Outside, the beach is still there just as it was yesterday, but different, too, just as it is different every day. The waves are folding gently in towards the shore. It is beautiful, and he imagines a flood tide that doesn't stop, that keeps coming, up underneath the house, up and up through the floorboards. He imagines the shoreline gone, pushed inland, the ocean devouring the land, and nothing but water there before his eyes. Leaning against the sink, he lets his head fold forward, looking at his hands, trying to block out the image in his mind.

Sharna is beside him. She puts her hands on his shoulders and turns him towards her. He lifts his head and sees that her eyes are glistening. 'I don't want to go either,' she says. 'I don't want to go.'

Out of the corner of his eye Niall sees Wendy walk out of the room. He pulls Sharna close. He feels his resistance crumbling. He remembers what she has been saying all these months, and finally he feels as though he understands. It is time to go. He is afraid to leave this place, afraid to leave the place that is so full of Sharna, afraid of what it will mean for them. But the ocean is not going to let them stay.

'It's okay,' he says. 'I'm sorry, I'm sorry. I'll come. We'll go together.'

They hold one another for a long time, leaning against the kitchen sink with the ocean rolling on endlessly outside the window.

Rollerbaby Queen

Venetia Di Pierro

Me and Gina, the roller-skating arcade baby-queen, sit out front under the ripped awnings of her daddy's shop. The rain pours down beyond; everything's damp, even the air around us. Our clothes hungrily soak up the smell of smoke as we steadily work our way through a stolen pack. I'm busy piffing marbles at a tin can out in the rain, and Gina kicks her skates against the pavement so the glitter wheels never get time to rest. Everyone knows Gina, she's everyone's girl really, but not really anyone's. I'd thought about kissing those fire-engine lips, but I'd seen her kick for less with her skates and they could bruise real bad. Besides, I got a thing for Darla – with the blonde hair from the bakery – that keeps me up at night, twisting, rumpling and sweating. She's eighteen and engaged to marry Pauly Salvatore's big brother – well that's what Gina said. Still, I couldn't help creeping down to the bakery every morning 'til Ma said, *How much damn bread could one family eat?* Gina knows most things that go on 'round here. *These streets,* she sometimes says, *they don't have no secrets from me. They whisper straight into the soles of my feet.*

I'm not sure how often her feet are out of those skates, but I believe her. I think those big brown eyes, too wise for a kid, seen lots of things most old men'll never know.

My last marble's sitting in the street, and there ain't much happening, so I ask Gina if she wants to walk down and get a cream puff, but she says no, she's wearing her gold sequin top and can't chance the rain. I suggest we go in and play billiards; she says okay, even though she's sick of that stupid game, sick to death. Gina's prone to dramatics, but I can see she's a bit down on account of the rain and no people around. I don't really care; I like having the joint to myself. If no one's around, usually Gina and me play games or she lets me skate around the stained red carpet between the tables, but sometimes, if it's real bad, Gina disappears. Her cousin Angelo stands behind the counter, drinking coffee and listening to the races on the radio. If he's nice, we get coffees, but if he's sour, he kicks me out. Today, he's okay, bored too maybe, and he sits while we play a game and tells us stories about the best fights he's been in.

The tables are all old, with faded, dusty felt, but we always play number three. You gotta know which cues are good, and which have the splinters. Once I got a piece of wood stuck so bad, Angelo pulled it out, but when I got home, my ma cried and said I had no hope. Why do women do that? You can't get nothing past her, even though you got your hands in your pockets she's still at you: *Wha's that? Why you hiding, Franky? Dio mio! Why you do these things?* Then she starts and I go to my room and turn on the radio.

But Gina and me, today Angelo makes us milkshakes – he never done that before. I feel proud, but Gina said, *He makes 'em no good,* and didn't care if he heard or not. She rolls from corner to corner on her skate-hardened brown legs, stuffed into her little sateen shorts, which are already giving at the sides, and flicks the ball with gusto, stooping to eyeball the correct colours into the pockets. She's good as most of the guys, but I'm not bad, even though Angelo keeps giving advice and pointing with the big end of a cue. Gina tells him to shut it, and he whacks her on the legs and laughs, not letting the toothpick fall from his thin lips. We stop to drink and smoke; I imagine I look bad like James Dean in *Rebel Without A Cause,* and Angelo says, *What's a shake without fries?* I'm in heaven. Gina cusses and rolls over to the mirror, which is really an ad for Marlboro, and puts more red on her lips, then adjusts her tiny boobs in the gold top, and says, *Angelo must be happy 'cause he got some last night.* She rubs lipstick off a big tooth – did I mention she has big teeth? Kinda a big mouth for her face – and I go a little pink in the face, knowing that Angelo coulda heard what she said. She turns her neck, weighed down by that curly brown ponytail that bounces and flips when she moves, and says, *You don't know nothin', kid.* Angelo puts down a basket of fries, with the paper already starting to grease up, and I say, *Thanks,* and he says, *Don't get no ideas about next time.* I set the balls up, but Gina says she's sick of wiping the floor with my ass, and yells to Angelo, who's back near the radio, to put on some nice music. I have some coins in my pocket, so I offer Gina to play the wizard pinball with me, but she tells me I should dance with her, even if I do have *the knobbliest knees outta any guy ever.* I don't wanna dance in the arcade, especially 'cause two of Angelo's friends come in with loud voices, so I sit at the wizard and try to make the game last long, dipping into the basket and hitting the buttons with my shiny, salt-crusted fingers. Gina gets distracted and rolls over to ply cigarettes and adult conversation. *Don't you dare turn the races back on, Ange, I like this song.* The friends laugh at her sass, which I can tell she likes, 'cause she lays it on real good now, like the little adult-girl sideshow she is. Everyone knows her, and treats her with the respect she demands, so she skates backwards, and blows smoke rings, calling the men *honey* and giving them advice until Angelo flicks her with a tea-towel and tells her to get out and play like a normal kid. No one minds that she's a kid in the game, 'cause she's been grown-up since she was born.

The rain has stopped and I hear the school bell. It

doesn't take long for the kids to straggle in, dumping soggy bags and pushing with their lanky, tanned arms and yelling above the noise. Everyone calls to Gina, and she sits on a lofty stool by the men, flicking her chin in acknowledgment when she can be drawn away from the testosterone talk rich with innuendo and ribbing. I know I'm forgotten for now, but the main boys from school spot me and fall on the rest of my fries like flapping pigeons. We pool our dough for a billiard tournament and Michael tells me Mr Haldrummer is ringing my ma 'bout too many skipped classes and I shrug, 'cause now I'm Jim Stark. Billy starts talking about Gina, like he always does; he's still sore 'cause he tried to put the moves on her when we were in Green's lot, but she laughed at him and ran over his foot. At first Billy had the paranoids about Angelo, but now he's just pissed. *Look at her, letting that old guy put his hands all over her. Whore.* I look. One of the men, the old men that come and drink their black coffees, has her perched on his knee, but he holds his cigarette out of reach of her grabbing hands, and pays her no mind. *Then forget her,* I say to Billy with the fat face. He takes his shot and misses the ball, then goes back to sullenly tracking Gina as she travels across to the older girls, popping gum in the side of her cheeks. She briefly looks at us, through us, and I know I'm no companion at all for her in a busy room. I don't care; I poke Billy in the ribs and make room for Pauly Salvatore, who pulls out a fresh pack, and I can tell he ain't been near school neither.

Evening comes, and the shop empties to the invisible dinner bell. I look for Gina, but she's gone. I go pee in the sticky floored restroom and push through the back door. I'm in no hurry to go home and listen to Ma's hysterics. Pap's belt will be waiting beside his plate on the table, so I know he knows. Out in the alley behind the arcade it's hot and muggy, still damp and stinks from the garbage cans. I pick a hardly smoked butt out of the ashtray that Angelo uses out here. That's when I notice Gina sitting on the bottom step. She hunches away from me. I wanna play it cool with her so she doesn't get in a mood, but I need her light. *Sure,* she sighs like a much older woman and swivels her knees to face me. There's a scrape on her shin and red scabs from scratched at mosquito bites. I look away before she can see me looking. *Still wanna get a cream puff?* I shake my head, even though I do, 'cause now my pockets are empty. She smiles over those big teeth and shakes her head a little. *What is it with you guys?* She stands. I watch her gold sequins disappear as the door flicks shut behind her.

She's All Broken

Peter R Hill

My name is Margaret. I dribble down my chin. That's embarrassing for a twenty-six-year old woman. My head lolls around, and when I try to speak my mouth emits alarming noises. Strange as it may seem, these disconcerting attributes, which you might expect would attract attention, more often than not render me invisible. People feel embarrassed. They have no idea how to deal with a wild-eyed young woman struggling to control her body. They assume that if my body is out of control then my brain must be in a similar state. There are times when this is useful.

The atrium of the National Gallery is buzzing with people. I'm not far from the entrance, sitting in my special motorised wheelchair. Adam has gone off to see an exhibition – supposedly. Adam's my minder. He's a good-looking guy in his thirties. My mind says that if my body wasn't such a mess, he's the sort of guy I'd fancy. Good-looking and caring. Anyone who chooses to give up his time to wipe dribble off the chin of a spastic must be caring. Of course, he never calls me spastic – political correctness, and all that.

But I digress. Adam has really gone off to meet his girlfriend for coffee. I don't mind. I can get around, and I like to watch people just as much as they like to ignore me.

Now I watch as a party of Chinese tourists comes through the doors. A young woman leads the way, her arm stretched high above her head, holding a little yellow flag. *Funny the flag's not red.* The security guard politely stops the group, and signals that those with bags should check them at the quaintly named *cloak counter.* The young woman relays the message in Chinese, shouting above the babble of the group.

A white couple have come through the doors behind the Chinese party. The woman is very attractive; her long coat swishes around her sexy tan boots. The couple detach themselves from the Chinese. The man has a bag over his shoulder. He's carrying a coat that he positions to cover the bag. He hangs back a fraction, following the woman as she walks around the Chinese throng. Now they are almost level with the security guard. I am willing him to turn around, and he does. He sees the woman and opens his mouth to say something. She smiles at him and laughs as she opens her coat cheekily and holds up a small purse on a strap. Her companion walks around the back of the distracted guard, his coat still covering the bag.

I am watching the guard, hoping that he will see the man and check that bag, but the woman is flirting with him, saying something, laughing, flicking her head so that her long hair dances and sways, like one of those shampoo ads. God knows what my hair looks like, hacked short for convenience and washed every four days by Mary, who visits the hostel. Mary is a Kiwi. She claims to be a hairdresser but we all reckon she's a shearer, now too old to toss sheep. We're as close as she can get to defenceless animals.

The man has walked across the open area and is about to turn into the ticketing annex for *The Cubists* exhibition. Another group of foreign visitors arrive, and the guard reluctantly turns away from the woman to deal with this buzzing swarm. She walks away, her demeanour turning serious as she strides across the tiled floor.

With the palm of my tortured hand I push the black lever that controls my wheelchair. The chair glides forward and I stop close to the guard. He's busy but I am determined to attract his attention. Desperately, I try to make 'excuse me' come out of my mouth. I emit a strange noise; it's enough to make him turn. He looks at me, somewhat startled, and I raise my bent arm and try to point to where the couple have gone.

'You're all right, love,' he says, and waves me away.

Another effort produces another beast-like sound, but the guard busies himself with new arrivals and ignores me. *Dopey bastard.*

So it's up to me. I head off in pursuit of the suspects, perhaps a little too fast for one old couple; they stop suddenly to avoid being knocked over by the mad woman in her wheelchair. The old guy mutters something uncharitable and I slow down in the hope that I can glide into the ticketing annex unnoticed. It's early; there are only a few people waiting for tickets. My head chooses a bad time to go feral and it takes me a minute or two to spot the couple. They are together at the ticket counter. The man is still using his coat to hide the bag. The woman leans into him and whispers. She looks serious; all her flirty acting of a few minutes ago is over.

So I have the enemy in sight, but I am not sure what to do. I wish Adam would appear; at least he would take some notice and eventually figure out what I was on about. But that would be a performance that would attract too much attention – me trying to talk while gesticulating to make Adam understand. It's like playing charades with someone who makes animal noises and has St Vitus dance.

They're on the move. They've got their tickets and are walking towards the exhibition entrance. Surely the attendant on the door will notice the bag and raise the alarm. The woman is up to her tricks again. She has positioned herself between her partner and the attendant – just half a step ahead. Her coat is open. I assume she has clothes on underneath, but, by the look on the attendant's face, perhaps not. He scans the proffered tickets without taking his eyes off her, all the time smiling broadly, totally oblivious to the existence of the man, who has walked on and joined the people gazing at the first of the paintings.

I get my shaking arm under some semblance of control and push the lever. My chair purrs forwards towards the exhibition entrance, squeezing ahead of a young couple. *Shit, I don't have a ticket.* The attendant looks down at me, then looks hopefully at the couple behind me. Then he looks back at me. His eyes have widened. He waves vaguely towards the open doors and moves quickly away to check the tickets of normal people. I'm inside. If I'd known it was so easy to get in without paying, I'd have come to all the exhibitions.

A well-intentioned man notices me and loudly asks people to move aside to allow me to see a painting. I'm trying to keep a low profile, yet he makes a scene, causing everyone to turn and look at me. I have no choice but to pretend I am admiring a Picasso painting. Actually, I do admire it. It's of a woman, but she's all broken, just like me. Perhaps this Picasso guy knew something about people like me. Although, in a TV documentary I saw, he had lots of women – all good-looking.

Mustn't get distracted. My eyes dart around looking for the couple. I can't see them. I manoeuvre my chair away from the group and make for the next room.

I cruise carefully into the room. It's not as busy in here, and I can see a security person sitting on a chair in the far corner. She looks bored, and is fiddling with a bracelet on her wrist. She's not making any attempt to scan the room for would-be thieves or terrorists. *Should I motor over and remonstrate with her?* No, that would be useless. With my luck, I'd be the one to get ejected.

This room has two doorways. I'll try the one on my right. *Damn.* The couple are coming out just as I'm going in. They stand aside to let me through. I'm the only one in a small room with no other exit. I move around the room. I'm keen to leave and follow the couple, but if I reappear too quickly I might arouse suspicion. I think I'm getting the hang of this detective stuff. Next to a painting that looks like a cat made from Lego, there is a gap where a picture has been; there's a small notice on the wall. I ease closer to read it. It's a bugger looking up all the time but I read the words:

Picasso's Weeping Woman has been returned to the Museé Picasso in Paris. It was on loan to the gallery until March 31ˢᵗ.

I missed it by a day. Strange, I thought the gallery had its own *Weeping Woman.*

I figure it's safe to head out again and I roll back through the doorway into the room with the security woman. It's got busier. I search for my suspects. I catch sight of the woman's boots through a forest of legs. Very expensive boots. I get a totally different view of the world from where I sit. I spend my life looking people in the crotch or the bum. The boots are moving towards the next picture. Where's the man? This is a forest of women's legs; there are no trousers.

I execute the closest thing to a pirouette in a wheelchair, slowly completing three-sixty degrees. I take in the whole room. I can't see the man. They must have split up.

Damn. The do-gooder is back.

'You all right, love? Can you see all right?'

I make my noise for 'yes' and try my best to nod and smile while frantically searching the room.

'Have you lost someone?'

Of course I've bloody lost someone, you halfwit, and I've no chance of finding him while you're holding me up. I manage to raise my left arm and wave it from side to side in the hope that he will read that as a 'No'. My recalcitrant right hand struggles to push the control lever forward and I take off, almost running over the Samaritan's foot. In the next room I scan the lines of people viewing the pictures. I can't see the man so I motor straight through. Looks like I'm in the last room of the exhibition. I can see the exit with an attendant standing by the door. I wheel around, desperately trying to keep my head pushed back against the head-rest. It's very hard to see anything when my neck gives up and my chin drops onto my chest.

There he is, moving along a line of pictures towards the exit. He's not pausing long enough to look at the works properly. *Shit!* The bag has gone. The coat he was using to conceal it is slung, Sinatra style, over his shoulder, a finger through the loop on the collar. He strolls past the attendant and out through the exit. Will I follow him? No point, he hasn't got the bag. I get myself under control. Where's the bag? I look along the floor by the walls. He wouldn't leave it on the floor. That would be too obvious – someone would pick it up or report it. I try to recall each of the rooms. I didn't notice any cupboards and I know there are no toilets in this area.

I turn and move slowly back towards the previous room, carefully searching for a place where they might have hidden the bag.

'Going back for another look, are we?'

Jesus, not again. This guy pops up more times than a meerkat. And if he wasn't annoying enough already, now he uses the royal 'we'.

I accelerate, and he moves to one side, still smiling. Some people still wouldn't get the message if you hit them with a lump of four-by-two.

As I re-enter the previous room I see the woman directly opposite, walking through the archway. Now I understand how she mesmerised the men. She's tall, elegant and beautiful. I hate her. Her coat is unbuttoned. I can't see the bag. *What's going on?* They must have hidden it somewhere. Wait a minute – there's another woman talking to her.

I turn my wheelchair towards the wall of paintings and pretend to be taking in the confusion of a picture of a woman and musical instruments – bits of both, all mixed-up, bent and weird. *Wow.*

The women are now moving together along a row of paintings. I turn away and slowly move back to the last room. I position myself in the middle so that I will be able to see the women when they enter. I am praying the do-gooder doesn't pop up again. Here they come, and there's the bag, it's over the shoulder of the new villain, an older woman, smartly presented with page-boy length blonde hair. She looks straight at me. I wheel my chair around so that I am facing the last of the paintings and the exit. *Of course, the exit. How do they plan to get past the attendant without him seeing the bag?*

The women are moving closer. I'll leave now so I don't distract the attendant, then there will be more chance he'll spot the bag. But they've moved quickly and must be close behind me. I feel something or someone touch the back of my wheelchair. I move through the exit; my head has fallen to my right, and I can see the older woman walking alongside me. I can't see the bag. Both women stay next to me as I leave the exhibition, as if they are with me. Once we are clear of the exit the older woman turns and reaches behind me. I feel some movement and see that she has the bag again. She laughs and says, 'Thanks, love.' She must have hung the bag on the back of my chair. Of course the drongo on the door didn't dare question me. The women stride off. I motor after them.

'Where've you been?' Adam appears in front of me, stopping my pursuit of the villains. I wave my left arm and make incoherent noises that cause people to turn and look at me. I need someone to look at the women.

'What is it, Margaret? What's the matter?' At least Adam knows I am agitated.

'Look, you're making a mess. Let me wipe your face.' Adam steps to the left to retrieve a towel from the basket on the back of my chair. I push the lever hard and make for the exit, more quickly than is safe. I can't see the women but if I can get outside I might be able to stop them.

'Hey!' Adam yells from behind me. Now we really do have an audience. A gallery security guard steps in front of me with his hand up.

'Stop!'

I manage to stop without hitting him. Adam has

caught up and grabs the handles of my chair.

'Is she with you?' the guard asks Adam. I make more noises and wave my flailing arms in the direction of the exit.

'You sure she should be in here?'

'She's normally fine. I don't know what's wrong.' Adam turns to me. He has the towel in his hand; he leans forward and wipes my face.

'What's got into you, Margaret? You'll get us thrown out,' he says quietly.

I look at him. I look at the exit then back at him.

'The bag,' I try to say, but I sound like a bleating sheep.

'Come on, I'll get you outside. We'll try to sort it out there,' he says. He starts to push the chair, but I jab the lever and scoot off towards the doors.

'Margaret!' Adam says. I can hear him running after me. The automatic doors are slow to swing open and I have an anxious moment with a cartoon vision of me, and the wheelchair, compressed against the glass. I head out into the sunlight and stop in the centre of the forecourt. A few people are coming and going, but I can't see the women.

Adam catches up. 'Margaret! That's enough. We're going home.' He's pissed off. How can I tell him what has happened? I start my charades act, but it's all too hard and Adam is not receptive. What would I tell him anyway … that I've been following a bag?

We're in a little semicircle, in our wheelchairs, in front of the TV, fighting with our food. The journey from plate to mouth is a hazardous one when your brain can't tell your limbs how to behave. Peter Hitchener starts the news.

'Police are investigating the theft of a painting from *The Cubists* exhibition at the National Gallery.' I choke, and food goes everywhere.

'A small painting was taken some time today. The thieves placed an official looking notice on the wall stating that the painting had been returned to the Picasso Museé in Paris. It appears that the CCTV camera was not working in the room where the painting was displayed.'

'Margaret, what have you done? Look at this mess.' Maureen starts to pick up the food that I've scattered across the floor. I'm waving both arms, trying to point at the television, but I only manage to hit the screen with the last of the potato from my fork.

'Margaret. Behave. Now look what you've done to that nice Mr Hitchener,' she says, as she wipes the TV with a napkin. She stops to look at the shot of Picasso's *Weeping Woman* that's now on the screen.

'What a funny picture,' she says. 'Can't imagine who'd want to steal that.'

Oh, Christ. I don't believe it.

'I saw them,' I try to say, waving my arms again. Maureen stands in front of me.

'What are you trying to tell us, Margaret?'

I feel like weeping.

The Human Child

Adrienne Tam

In my dream, I am a child again, no more than eight years old. I'm back at home, in the village, standing in the yard behind the family house. Everything burns with colour. The sky is a rich indigo. The grass is as green as my mother's emerald ring.

But the woods at the edge of the property are a monstrous black. The *baka* trees seem to be creeping forward, eating up the ground as they move towards me. I want to run into the house and bury my face in my mother's skirts, but my feet are rooted to the spot. The sky is growing darker now, and all the colour is leaving the world.

Suddenly Sam bursts out of the woods, his chubby two-year-old legs running as fast as they can. He looks frightened, and something terrible blooms in my stomach; I have never known my brother to be afraid of anything. I yell at him to run faster. The black tide is nipping at his heels. I want to go to him, to pick him up and carry him, but I still can't move.

As he runs, the yard grows longer, and he gets further and further away. I pull hard against the forces keeping me in place and all at once I'm running towards him, screaming his name. I know I'm growing older as I run, the way these things are known in dreams. By the time I reach the middle of the yard, now the size of two rugby fields, I am my normal twenty-four-year-old self.

Sam is growing older too. He grows and grows until he is taller than me, until he's the eighteen-year-old boy whom I do not recognise anymore. It's been so long since I have looked upon his face.

We're barely five feet away from each other when the branches of the *baka* trees reach forward and wrap around Sam's feet. He screams at me to help him, and I try, I try so hard, and for one eternal moment my fingers brush against his, but the branches are too strong and too quick and they sweep Sam off his feet, pulling him into their black embrace.

I wake up screaming.

My mind tries to dislodge itself from the nightmare and back into the real world as I fumble and flail in bed. My heart is thundering and my hair's matted with sweat, as if I really did run the length of those two rugby fields. The clock on my bedside table reads 3.21am.

A loud ringing noise shatters the silence. I let out a muffled scream, which quickly dissolves into a hysterical laugh-sob when I realise it's just my phone. Grabbing it from the bedside table, I frown at the screen. It's a private number. For a moment I consider not picking up, even though the call must be important, given the time.

There's a deep sense of foreboding, of something rushing towards me.

'Hello?' I say into the phone.

'Kesa? That you?' a woman's voice comes over the line.

'Who is this?'

'Kesa,' the woman says. 'It's Ari.'

Ari. Arieta. My big sister, whom I'd not spoken to in a little over seven years. My heart picks up speed.

'Ari,' I say. 'What–? How–?'

'I got your number from Mesake's mum. I know it's late but I need to speak to you.' There's no 'How are you?' or 'It's good to hear your voice'. I don't expect there to be, not after how I left, but the part of me that loves my sister dies a little.

'It's about Sam,' Ari continues.

For a moment, I see Sam being pulled back into the woods.

'Sam? What about Sam?'

'He's gone missing,' Ari says.

'What do you mean, gone missing? What happened?'

'I don't know, exactly. It's been three days and we still haven't heard from him, and Ma is … she's not doing so good. She asked for you.'

The angry words I was ready to say – *Three days? He's been missing three days and you only tell me* now? – stick in my throat.

'She did?' I whisper.

'Yes. We were wondering if you could … if you could come back. Here. Home.'

Home. I remember home. I remember Ma's vegetable garden in the front yard and the red letterbox held together by mismatched wood and superglue. The way my father used to sweep through the front door after work with mud on his clothes and the way Sam and I used to race home from school, Ari following behind at a more dignified pace. I remember the smell of the soil and the woods, and the sound of hymns on Sunday mornings.

'Okay,' I say. My voice is resolute despite the trepidation I feel. 'Okay.'

The bus travelling from Suva to Tavua is so old I half expect it to break down as soon as the driver turns on the engine. It splutters and coughs like a chain smoker before settling into a deep rumble that never lets up during the entire eight hour ride.

I'm squashed in my seat by a large Rotuman woman wearing a wide-brimmed hat, and who smells of pineapples. I try to sleep but the air is stifling and the road is riddled with potholes and there's a baby crying in the seat behind me.

I remember Sam as a baby, how tiny and red he was, how all he seemed to do was sleep. Even though he didn't cry and he loved to smile, I hadn't liked him at first. In my six-year-old eyes, my brother was a nuisance, a small thing that took up entirely too much attention.

Then one day my mother had plonked Sam in my arms and told me to look after him.

'You're the big sister now,' she had said.

I had looked down at Sam. He had large brown eyes, and he smelled of baby powder. When I poked his nose experimentally, he reached up with his small hand and gripped my finger.

'He loves you best, I think, Little Bit,' my father had said.

Another death rattle from the bus accompanied by a hard nudge from the Rotuman woman pulls me from my memories, and I'm surprised to find tears at the corners of my eyes.

Ari is waiting at the main bus station. A man I recognise from the wedding photos as her husband stands beside her. I dismiss the husband for the moment, focusing all my attention on my sister. She's thicker in the waist than I remember, which makes sense given the two children she's borne. Her long dark hair is still long and dark, but perhaps not as lustrous. Her face, though older, is still so beautiful, and I feel the familiar awe in the presence of my sister's beauty.

'Ari,' I say, not sure what to do.

'Hello, Kesa,' she says, and pulls me in for a brief hug. I blink furiously at the sudden sting in my eyes.

'This is Temo, my husband,' Ari says when we break apart. I shift my attention to him. He is a very tall man, with hands that are as big as my head. He smiles politely at me and we shake hands.

'It's nice to meet you,' I say, and the tall man nods solemnly. I'm reminded of a time when I was seven and Ari was eleven and we were in our mother's room trying on her make-up.

'When I grow up, I'm going to wear make-up every day,' Ari had said.

'Me too.'

'And my husband will tell me I'm beautiful every day.'

'What will your husband look like?'

'He'll be very handsome, like Pa. He'll have nice eyes. And tall, he'll be very tall.'

Something of the memory must have shown on my face because when Ari's eyes meet mine, there's a hint of amusement in them.

At first the drive to the village is silent. Temo drives expertly along the dirt road, manoeuvring through the darkness and potholes with ease.

'Have the police said anything?' I ask after a while.

Ari's voice is hard when she answers. 'They're useless. It took them two days to even come out to the house. And then all they did was ask questions instead of getting out there and actually *looking* for him. They think he ran away to Suva. Like all the other kids.'

Like you. The words, unspoken, hang heavy between us.

'He'd never run away,' I say.

'How would you know?' she bristles. 'It's been a long time since you spoke to him. Things aren't the same, you know. He's grown up.'

'He wrote to me.' I shrug casually even though I feel a certain vindictive thrill.

'What?'

'Yeah. Sometimes it would be six, seven months before I heard from him. But he wrote. He sent me your wedding photos.' In the dark of the van, I see Temo's left hand close over Ari's right. It goes quiet once again.

'So, no one saw anything the night he disappeared?' I break the silence.

'Nothing. His bed was rumpled, so he must have slept in it. There wasn't anything missing from his room. He'd just ... vanished.'

It's almost eleven by the time the car arrives at Veikoso. As there are no roads through the village, we park at the entrance and continue to the house on foot. It's darker out here than it is in the city. As we walk, I catch glimpses of soft figures moving against windows lit up by candlelight and the glint of an animal's eyes in the moonlight. There's a *yaqona* session happening somewhere; I can hear laughter and the faint strum of a guitar.

We cross through Mr Vatulele's plantation and suddenly the house is just *there*, pouncing out of the dark like a monster. The front door is open, as usual. The only time it's ever closed is when we're asleep.

'I'll see you at home,' Temo says to Ari, and with a jolt, I realise my sister no longer lives in the family home; she is a woman now, with a house and family of her own. Temo turns to me. 'Goodnight, sister.' He gives me a small smile before being swallowed up by the night.

Ari picks up a lantern on the doorstep and lights it. She leads me through the house, stopping now and again to point something out, as if I'm a stranger, and the wrongness of the gesture makes me angry. I may not have been welcome in this house for years, but I have slept here and fought here and lived here.

'I don't need a tour,' I say.

Ari's eyes are flint. 'Come, then. Ma's outside.'

The blackness of the night is all-consuming in our backyard. The only light in the world seems to come from the glow of the lantern in Ari's hand, and even then the brightness of that light is dimmed in the face of all the darkness around us. The woods loom large at the edge of our property, the tops of the trees reaching up into the sky.

Ma sits in the middle of the yard, some six or seven feet away from where the woods begin, her back to us. When I draw alongside her, I see the way her eyes track the woods' border, back and forth, searching the shadows. She looks smaller, more fragile, more wounded than the last image I have of her: standing tall in our living room, finger pointing theatrically to the open door. It would have been funny had it not been so heartbreaking.

Go! After all I have done for you. What would your father say? Go then! Never come back! You hear me? Never come back!

And I went, and I told myself I would not return, not until the stars fell from the sky and the world neared its end. But I'd been young then, only seventeen, and time changes everything, even a hardened heart. Or maybe the world is just ending.

'Hello, Ma,' I say, crouching beside the still form. She doesn't acknowledge me.

'Kesa,' Ari says. 'Ma's been … acting a bit strange since Sam disappeared.'

I frown. 'What do you mean?' I reach out and shake Ma's arm. 'Mama?'

She blinks and turns to me. 'Have you seen him?' she whispers. Her first words to me after seven years, and the subject is someone else. I feel a horrible, fleeting envy of my brother.

'No, Ma,' I say. 'But we'll find him.'

She stares at me for a few more seconds before turning her gaze back to the woods.

I look at Ari accusingly. 'What's wrong with her?'

'Let's talk about this inside,' Ari says, reaching for Ma's arm. 'You should come back inside now, Ma. Come and have some tea; it's cold out here.'

'No, I have to wait for him,' she replies. Her voice is soft, hopeful. 'He'll come home soon. You go. Leave the light, maybe he'll need it.'

'What's she talking about?' I demand. 'What's wrong with her?'

Ari shakes her head. 'I don't know,' she says, but the words don't match her eyes.

'Kesa?' Ma says, turning to me. There is awareness in her gaze now. 'Is that you?'

'Yes, Ma, it's me. It's me.' I touch her hair, her face, her shoulders.

'You came back.' She places a hand against my cheek and I lean into it. This feels like forgiveness, this feels like home.

'Of course I did,' I say. An army of words marches up my throat and out my mouth. 'I'll always come if you call me. I'm so sorry, Ma. I never meant to hurt you. I never meant to hurt *any* of you. I just wanted … I just *wanted*. I'm so sorry.'

She continues to caress my cheek, a faraway smile on her face. Suddenly the smile falls. 'You shouldn't have come back,' she says, removing her hand. Her voice is cold and empty now. 'I told you never to come back.'

An abnormally large bird flies out of the woods, blacker than night. It passes over us with a loud caw and I remember what Sam used to say.

The word of a bird is a thing to follow.

'They're watching us, you know,' Ma says. Both Ari and I turn to look at her. 'They're right there, can't you see?' She points at the woods and I can't help staring in the direction of her finger. I'm afraid and I don't know why.

'There's nothing there, Ma,' Ari says. 'Let's get inside.' She leans down again to grasp Ma's arm and suddenly Ma is screaming in her face, a terrible piercing shriek that causes Ari to fall back, lantern shattering against the ground.

A flare of hot, white-blue light illuminates us for a moment as the kerosene from the lamp mixes with the fire. Later that night, I would tell myself I was mistaken, but in that brief instant, I see a figure standing between the trees by the edge of the woods, a shadow of a shadow.

Then the fire relents, and darkness falls once again.

My eyes blur, trying to adjust. Ma is still screaming, clawing at the grass and the soil beneath. Ari stomps out the last meagre flames of fire and leans down to pull her away, but she is strengthened by madness and can't be moved.

'Help me!' my sister says to me, and the command unfreezes my limbs. Together, we grip Ma's arms and drag her across the yard and into the house, shutting the door firmly behind us.

It takes more than an hour to get Ma to calm down. Ari does most of the work, soothing her with soft touches and even softer words until at long last the terrible screaming stops, and is replaced by nonsensical babbling – *so dark down there, my poor, poor baby* – which gradually tapers out as she falls asleep.

The screaming has drawn the attention of some of the neighbours, including Temo. I shake my head at him and he nods in understanding, practically frog-marching the neighbours away, telling them there is nothing to see here and to go back to their homes. My sister has found a good man.

'Here,' I say, pressing a hot cup of tea into Ari's hands.

We sit in silence for a while, eyes on the rise and fall of Ma's chest. The room smells like camphor oil. One of my earliest memories is of my mother sitting on the floor, massaging the oil into her feet after a long day at the markets.

'How long has she been like this?' I ask.

'Since Sam disappeared,' Ari answers. 'She sits outside every night, watching those damn woods. She keeps saying he's in the woods.'

'Have you looked?'

'Yes. Me, Temo and some of the villagers did a search. Nothing.'

Ma lets out a soft moan, and Ari pets her hair until she quietens.

'Do you remember when Sam was little and Ma thought he was cursed?' Ari asks, not looking at me.

I remember. It happened when Sam was two years old. His good nature had flown out the window seemingly overnight. He had cried and screamed and pulled his hair. He didn't want to be carried and he didn't like being sung to. He didn't speak and he didn't laugh. He was taken to the hospital in Tavua and the doctors ran a series of rigorous tests on him, but they could find nothing wrong.

Ma thought it was a *draunikau,* a curse, and the witchdoctor was called to the house to dispel the demon from Sam. Ari and I weren't allowed to watch the exorcism, but when we returned to the house the next day Sam was still howling like the wind during a cyclone, so we knew it hadn't worked. The village descended into rumour and gossip, and I heard snatches of conversation here – *not even his son; remember when she made eyes at Tevita? I always thought* – and there – *get him out of the village, I mean, it's just not natural for* – and the kids at school started calling Ari and me names.

I remember taking Sam from his cot one day while my mother slept and running to the woods behind our house.

'Sam,' I cooed to the boy as he cried. 'Please stop. They'll take you away, don't you see? Please, I love you, okay? Just be a good boy, Sam. Be a good boy.'

And just like that he stopped. He gazed at me, his eyes still large and brown, but there was something unsettling about his stare, something old, something *knowing*. The sun ducked behind the clouds and the woods went darker, colder. For a moment, I was actually frightened of my brother; for a moment I almost thought, *This isn't Sam,* but then he leaned into me and put his small arms around my neck and I hugged him tight, shivering. His touch was so cold.

'Yeah, I remember,' I say to my sister.

She's quiet for a moment. 'There's something I haven't told anybody. Ever.' She looks at me. 'Not ever. Not Temo or Ma, nobody.'

I nod, my heart beginning to beat faster. 'Okay.'

I watch her swallow hard. 'When Sam was little, I used to check in on him at night, sit with him for a little while,' she says. 'I just … I know he loved you the best, but sometimes I just … I wanted him for myself too.' I feel a pang at those words and open my mouth to say something, but Ari shakes her head.

'One night, the night before Sam … started acting strangely, I went to his room,' she continues. 'Everyone was sleeping. It was late, after midnight, I think. I noticed the room was kind of cold, and I saw the window was open, so I went to close it.' She holds my gaze. 'And I saw something. Something outside, just outside the window.'

Goosebumps break out on my arms. 'What did you see?'

'A monster,' she says, flatly. 'There was a monster outside. It was small, like a dwarf, and it was shaped like a man, but its body was black and twisted, and it walked weirdly, like … like it wasn't used to it. It was carrying something, but I couldn't see what it was. It was walking away, towards the woods, but it must have sensed me or something, because it turned to look at me. And its face, dear God, Kesa, its face …' She begins to cry and I pull her into an embrace.

'Sshh,' I say, rocking our bodies to and fro. 'It's okay, it's okay.' For the first time in my life, I feel like the older sister; I feel like the stronger one.

It doesn't take long for Ari to pull herself together.

She looks embarrassed by her crying as she wipes her nose in the folds of her *sulu*.

'Do you know the changeling story?' she asks.

'Changeling?' Scraps of childhood fairytales come to mind. 'You mean, that story about fairies who exchange their fairy child for a human one? What's—?'

It was carrying something, but I couldn't see what it was.

'No,' I say. Ari does not look at me. I feel myself go pale. 'No,' I say again. 'You're wrong. Whatever you think you saw, you're wrong.' She flinches.

It was carrying something.

Without another word, I leave the room.

The next few days are strained. Ma is sometimes fully cognizant and then she slips back into an almost child-like madness. Ari does her best to take care of her, but her husband and children need her attention too, so I try to be the one Ma relies on. Despite her aversion to doctors, I manage to convince Ma, in a rare moment of lucidity, to allow one to check her over. The doctor diagnoses her condition as a temporary psychotic break, most probably due to the trauma of Sam's disappearance. There is nothing we can do but be patient, and allow her to come back to us in her own good time.

Nothing makes sense. The police still have no leads on Sam. Ma is halfway crazy. Ari and I refuse to talk about the revelations from the other night. It's as if by not speaking about it, the entire incident could be erased. I long for my life in the city, where everything is stable and ordered.

'Kesa?'

I glance up from my book. I've been sitting with Ma for a good two hours now, keeping an eye on her as she stares up at the ceiling, mouthing words to it in silent conversation.

'Yes, Ma?'

'Are you married?'

I blink. 'No, I'm not.'

'Your pa and I were married for eighteen years. God rest his soul.'

'I know, Ma.'

She turns her gaze from the ceiling to me. 'You were gone a long time.'

Putting the book down, I shift to sit beside her on the bed. 'Yes. But I'm here now. I'm back.'

She hums a little. 'Sam will come back too. I saw him go into the woods, but he'll come back.'

'You saw him?'

'Yes. On that night. Something woke me up. I don't know what it was – maybe the back door? I don't know. I looked outside from there,' she says, pointing to the window by the bed, 'and I saw him walking through the yard, into the woods. I called him and he turned to look at me, but there was nothing in his face. Nothing.'

The unsettled feeling in my stomach grows stronger. 'What do you mean there was nothing in his face?'

'There was nothing. It was him, but it wasn't.'

'Why didn't you say something earlier?' I ask. 'Ari said nobody saw anything that night.'

'I just remembered. Everything's all jumbled in my head. I can't … I can't–'

Patting her hair, I shush her. 'It's okay, never mind, it's okay.'

Ma reaches for my hand, her dark eyes boring into mine. 'I'm sorry too, you know. I was so angry with you. I should never have told you not to come home.'

Bowing my head, I caress the hand in mine.

'Be careful,' Ma says. I look up to find her eyes once more on the ceiling and I know she has gone again. Her voice is almost robotic. 'Be careful. There are monsters in the woods.'

The trees are pulling Sam into their embrace. He is reaching for me, and for one eternal moment, our fingers brush against each other.

Help me, he says, and I pray to God for His mercy.

But it's too late. I wake up with Sam's name on my lips. My heart is thundering. I lie in the dark, wishing for morning. I want to smell the sun in the soil, and hear the village come alive. Morning would chase away all these shadows.

A sound comes from downstairs. It is soft, barely perceptible. It sounds like a door opening. I frown. Ari and I put Ma to sleep a while ago and she had been strangely acquiescent, despite the interruption to her nightly routine of sitting in the backyard. Surely she's not going outside at this hour, I think.

Slipping out of bed, I light the lantern and make my way to Ma's room. I open her bedroom door. She's sound asleep, her face turned towards me, soft snores escaping her mouth. Slowly, I head downstairs. The front door is closed. I move through the living room into the kitchen.

The back door is wide open. Lifting the lantern higher, I peer from the back door out into the yard, but I can't see very far. The stars are not out tonight. I close the door softly, making sure to click the lock into place. As I walk back through the living room to my bedroom, I feel a prickle in my spine, and a heavy dread comes over me. I stop in the middle of the living room.

From the shadows cast on the floor by the lantern in my hand, I can see there is someone standing directly behind me. I stop breathing. Terror has me rooted to the spot, binding my feet into the ground. I have never been so frightened in all my life, not even when my father had died and we were told to cover up all the mirrors in the house to stop his dead soul from coming back to haunt the living.

The person behind me leans in and I smell soil and trees. My fists are clenched so tight I am certain I'm drawing blood.

Kesa, the person says, and even though the voice is all wrong, even though it's high like a bird's chirp, I know it's Sam. Ma was right. He has come home. When I spin around, there's no one there. I race back to the kitchen. The back door is open once again.

The word of a bird is a thing to follow.

'Sam!' I scream, running through the yard to the woods. 'Sam!'

The woods are dark, but the light from the lantern stops me from falling over and bumping into the trees.

'Sam!' I scream again. I pause, listening. Everything is still, caught between breaths. The lantern's fire goes out abruptly and I let it drop to the ground with a curse. My eyes try to adjust to the gloom. For some reason, I'm unafraid, even though I was terrified mere seconds ago. Sam is out here, and I will not go home without him. A slight rustle comes from the right, and I blink in that direction.

'Sam?' I can make out the shape of someone standing a few feet away from me. 'Come home, Sam. Please come home,' I say, taking a step forward.

Another figure separates from the darkness and stands beside Sam. They are the same height. They have the same leanness.

It was carrying something but I couldn't see what it was.

Do you know the changeling story?

I remember Sam the baby, gripping my finger with his little hand. Sam the two-year-old, angry and spiteful and cold, but still looking at me as if he loved me best. Sam at five, not speaking to any of his classmates at kindergarten. Sam at eight, eyes too old and knowing. Sam at eleven, watching quietly from the doorway as I packed my bags for my life in the city.

My legs buckle and I fall to the ground.

'Sam,' I whisper and then I start crying. I don't know who I'm crying for: my parents, Ari, myself, Sam. Sam, the changeling; Sam, the human child. They are both my brother. A hand touches my neck as I kneel there, head bowed. The hand rests at my nape for a long while. The touch is cold.

Then he is gone.

The next morning burns blue and bright. I lie in my bed while the roosters crow and the dogs bark. In the light of day, the events of the previous night seem unreal, dream-like. But there's mud on my feet and dried tear tracks on my face. The ache is still there in my chest and I know it will be a constant thing now, a grief I will have to bear for the rest of my life.

Because my brother is never coming home.

I go outside and find Ma and Ari sitting in the backyard, eating buttered bread dipped in tea. I sit down next to them. Ari offers some of her bread and I accept it with a smile. Ma touches my arm fleetingly, eyes still darting towards the edge of the woods.

'Will you stay a while?' Ari asks.

Overhead, a bird calls.

'Yes,' I say. 'I'll stay.'

The Regatta

Luke Thomas

Two months in Africa without a shirt. The upper half of his body has tanned from standing up through the open top of the safari vehicle on the Serengeti Plain, and since arriving in Malawi the tan has deepened so that at night when he removes his shorts to shower there's a definite line at his waist separating the brown upper body from the pale lower half. He's a glowing picture of health. Tanned, toned and relaxed. He's shirtless again this morning, barefooted, drinking Elephant beer beneath a grass-roofed hut on the shores of a vast lake he's seen for the first time in his life and probably never will again.

But Tom's appearance belies the fact that he hasn't taken a solid shit in three weeks. Maybe it's all the beer and the sun, the dehydration, or perhaps the local food that has upset his guts so violently. Certainly the water wouldn't help. He's been warned to drink only bottled water, brush his teeth with it, and refuse ice cubes. But he could have slipped up along the way with all the beer and the sun and the dehydration. What about malaria? Do you shit Jackson Pollock rip-offs with malaria? If not malaria, then it could be any number of the strange

African diseases Tom couldn't spell even if he could name half of them.

Or maybe, just maybe, could it be his body's violent protest to the realisation that he may just hate his wife? He hasn't always hated her, of course. It's a recent discovery, no doubt induced by pitching a tent. Once or twice would be no problem. Tents by design are simple affairs. Any idiot can work it out. And they often do. But the act repeated forty-seven times over the past few months is wearing thin. Tom can see the result from where he sits at the camp bar this morning. Their tent is misshaped and sagging in the middle, up on a bare patch of rocky ground sloping into a ditch.

They'd fought three days ago, pitching it in the dark. Kate was unconvinced about the position and the evenness of the ground while Tom, tired and cramping and muttering curses under his breath, bashed in the pegs with the mallet. She let the torch wander for only a second, distracted by a rustling in the scrub behind her, and in that instant Tom bashed his thumb instead of a corner peg. He called out *Bitch!,* tossed the mallet into a nearby thicket, and although he wasn't directly referring to Kate, he didn't bother to defend himself because she called him a *fucking arsehole* and stormed off with the torch to the dining hut.

Tom let her go without a word. He seethed in the

dark alone. On cue, his guts began to churn and he left the mallet in the thicket, their tent loosely pitched, and stumbled his way through the darkness to the camp toilet block. A stall was free, the last in the row. Tom sat, sweated, and out of self-conscious embarrassment and friendly consideration for his stall neighbours, he employed clench and slow release tactics to muffle the explosive echo.

To complicate matters, Tom's convinced Kate fancies one of the blokes on tour. Joe is Swedish, blond, fit, and tans in the way only Scandinavians can tan. With his naturally unblemished skin, smooth and without a trace of a freckle or a mole, he dips each day, it seems, into a gradually darkening vat of hot caramel.

Why is this? The Swede's skin is nothing like Tom's Australian skin, his Queensland skin, his pale and blotchy inheritance. Tom blames his Welsh ancestors, a fair-freckled bunch who decided a hundred and twenty years ago to jump on a boat and sail to a scorched southern land. What were they thinking? Did they know the indigenous people were as dark as any African?

Tom burns before he tans. It's severe and painful. He

has to work at it. He has to be patient. He'll get there this time. He'll continue to keep his shirt off, use as little sunscreen as possible, and hope melanoma decides to make an exception.

Tom hasn't said anything to Kate about Joe. That would be a mistake. Things are fragile enough between them at the moment without accusing her of a wandering eye. But he *has* seen the photos on their digital camera. As is expected of every twenty-something abroad, they've not only documented the typical images of each destination during the day – in this case, grazing zebra on the African plains, elephants, lions, giraffe, and the *traditional* Masai warriors dressed in their red blankets, Nike runners, and Omega wristwatches – but the equally proportionate nights of drinking in campsites and hostel bars.

The party shots are all there without question. They are smiling and laughing and dancing. They are glassy-eyed, sunburnt, half-naked, arms thrown around one another, arms thrown around friends who, only a day or a week before, had been complete strangers. They are having the time of their lives on a strange and exotic continent. The photos *can't* lie. Can they? They have done their duty as backpackers, captured the images to share with friends back home, to post on Facebook. Some will be impressed. Some will envy them.

That's the whole point, isn't it?

But it's the pictures taken a couple of days ago, when Kate went horse riding around the lake without Tom, that stirs the most suspicion. The photos themselves reveal no damning evidence. Most are of Kate. It's around midday. The sky is clear, the sand to the shore of the lake white-hot and the water opal-blue. Kate is wearing her new black string bikini, the one that shows off her breasts, and she is smiling a smile Tom has forgotten ever existed. One photo has her looking back at the camera, hair whipped by a breeze, as the black mare she rides canters along the shore. The image is blurred by movement, glaring sunshine, and by the hooves of the mare as they kick up spray in the shallow water.

It's a good shot, Tom has to admit, the sun-flooded type plastered in travel agent windows advertising fun and exotic destinations to fit and happy people. But the only question Tom wants answered is, Who took it? Maybe he's paranoid. Maybe he's reading too much into it. Or maybe it's just the malaria medication finally kicking in, scrambling his brain. The doctor *did* warn him there would be side effects. Tom doesn't know. All he knows is that the last shot taken in the sequence that afternoon is of Joe with his back to the camera. Shirtless, Scandinavian-brown, broad-shouldered and astride a black mare of his own, Joe is washed with golden light and gazing off across the water to the sunset beyond.

To anyone else it would be a beautiful shot, a pretty thing to look at. But for Tom it's close to heartbreak, a betrayal. It's the type of romantically lurid picture Kate would have once taken of him.

Tom's sitting at the camp bar this morning with two other Australians. He hasn't planned it. It's just the way it goes. No matter where you are in the world, he's learned, in the biggest city or the smallest village, you are bound to bump into other Aussies. You hear the accent first, that nasal twang and that laboured drawl, and you shudder. You are repulsed by it and yet you are drawn to it. It's always just that little bit too loud, too abrasive, too shamelessly *Australian*, and, you think, shaking your head, do *I* sound like that?

These Aussies are two brothers from Adelaide, and just like Tom, they are shirtless, working on tans and thirsty for Elephant beer. They're about his age, late twenties, maybe a few years younger. They smile often, laugh, and share a story, a joke, an observation, with the carefree vulgarity of single men. Tom drank with them last night until the camp bar closed and they told him stories about pig shooting in Turkey, whores in Tokyo, mushroom shakes in Laos, and psychedelic shamans in South American jungles. Tom has his own stories to tell about the places he and Kate have seen in the last few months but they seem anaemic in comparison. The stories of two Aussie brothers drinking and fighting and fucking their way across oceans and continents were difficult to beat.

Mostly he listened. Mostly he nodded and he laughed.

Today the Brothers have organised a boat race on the lake – a regatta. They've hired the catamarans, the life jackets. They've set a course and the rules. There will be four catamarans, each with a team of two men. Out and around the island about a kilometre offshore, a small island, just some rocks sticking out of the water. First team back to the bar is the winner. There is even a trophy, a dark wood carving about a foot tall of a stooped African man, commissioned this morning from a souvenir stall in the nearby village. The legs and arms are disproportionately thin, the head large and cartoon-like, long flat nose, bug eyes, enormous lips. Across the bulging belly, carved into the dark wood, reads *Malawi Cup*.

Tom's up for it. He's keen for some action. It will give him a chance, at least for an hour or so, to forget about Kate. He stares out to the lake from his stool at the bar, drinks his one-dollar Elephant beer, rubs his tan chest, and wonders how paradise can be so underwhelming.

With the exception of the regatta in an hour there will be two more days of sitting around Lake Malawi drinking, smoking, shitting, before they all board the overland truck and head off for Victoria Falls. Tom's sure bitching in a place like this must be against the law, an offense punishable by flogging, but idleness and paranoia, no matter *where* you are in the world, is a fucking killer. He knows nothing about sailing, doesn't know a keel from a kaleidoscope, a tack from a toenail. But it hardly seems to matter.

The Brothers are paired together. Two Americans – two Floridians – make up the second team. They have accepted the challenge, forgoing a couple of sets of their daily volleyball game. The third team is a couple of English lads from Liverpool. Then there's Tom and Phil, the only team of mixed nationalities. Phil is a New Zealander and the Brothers are horrified.

How could you? He's like the enemy!

What are you talking about? Tom says. What about the ANZACS? Didn't we storm the beaches at Gallipoli side by side? Didn't we take Lone Pine? Chunuk Bair?

That's different, the Brothers reply in unison, anticipating his response.

That was war, one of them says.

This is *far* more important, says the other. This is *sport!*

Phil wasn't Tom's first choice. Nothing against the bloke, but he was getting desperate. After scouting for potential partners from one end of camp to the other this morning, Phil was the only one vaguely interested.

Phil was sitting with his wife in the shade of a thatched hut, fiddling with his camera, a serious-looking machine, the telescopic lens about a foot long. Phil's wife was sipping lemonade and highlighting passages from a *Lonely Planet*. Phil looked across at his wife before answering and she peered up from her book, smiled, and nodded approval.

Sure, Phil said. Why not?

Tom's only spoken to Phil a few times. Phil's a quiet bloke, and keeps pretty much to himself, or rather, keeps pretty much to his wife. Phil is a little more sensible than the other blokes on safari. He doesn't smoke the cheap local cigarettes, *any* cigarettes for that matter, and no one's ever seen him with a beer in his hand during the day. He wears a wide-brimmed hat whenever he's out in the sun. Khaki cargo pants instead of board shorts. Hiking boots instead of thongs. He's rarely without a shirt, but when he is, his body is pale and streaked with about sixteen layers of heavy-duty sunscreen.

Phil's here to have a good time. *Experience* Africa. His collection of safari shots is by far the best on tour. No surprise with the equipment *he's* packing. But Phil and his wife don't get into the party thing too much, the all day and all night drinking, the *serious* part of backpacking. Sure, they have a couple of drinks a night in the bar hut. They mingle and smile and chat, play a few hands of whatever card game is underway at the long table, but more often than not they are the first to leave. They return their glasses to the bar, wish everyone a goodnight, and disappear into the darkness together.

Their tent is pitched well away from the light and the noise of the bar. Tom's noticed it on his regular trips back and forth to the toilet block. The ground is flat and lush with grass in that part of camp. There are baobab trees to shield the morning light. And the tent, erected with precision and care, is a textbook example of outdoor living. Each of the twelve pegs is driven flush with the earth. The poles are steadfast pillars, the guy lines taut as guitar strings. The roof and the walls are seemingly spirit-levelled and made of harder stuff than canvas.

The fly could shrug off a hurricane.

Weak Northeaster, Phil says, zipping his lifejacket. Not much good for the run out. We'll have to take a wide line.

So you *do* know how to sail? Tom says, poking an

elbow into Phil's ribs.

Sure, he says coolly, as if every New Zealander was born with a rudder up their arse. I'm a member of a yacht club back home.

Standing on the shore of the lake, they look out to the island. It's hot and bright and they squint against the glare. A crowd is gathered behind them. The Americans quit their volleyball game a set earlier than usual and the English girls, for the first time in a week, are out of their deckchairs before sunset. A group of locals from the nearby village are assembled on a rise beyond the camp fence, staring down at the scene through the wire, pointing and laughing as if witnessing the curious habits of a strange and exotic species of animal.

Tom glances down the line at the Brothers, the English lads, the Americans. They're serious about this. They're crouched for the sprint down the beach to the catamarans.

What do I do? Tom asks. Where do I sit?

You jump in the front, Phil says. I'll take the back. Don't worry. Once we get going I'll tell you what to do.

The younger of the Australian Brothers calls from the far end of the line, You're welcome to give up now, girls! You're no chance! Prepare to be smashed!

Bullshit! replies one of the Americans. Pete and I'll be on our second beer by the time you pussies have reached the island!

One of the Liverpool lads pipes up. You've forgotten one thing! For two centuries the British were the Masters of the Sea!

Eat shit! is the reply.

One of the English girls, a blonde, has volunteered as the official starter of the race. Without a flag, she improvises by removing her bikini top and raising it above her head. Cheers and wolf-whistles erupt along the beach. On the hill, the locals howl, point and laugh with heightened intensity. Tanning oil glistens on the girl's body, everywhere except for on her bare breasts, two sharp-lined triangles, pale and severe against the new-brown of her tan.

Tom scans the beach for Kate. He hasn't seen her since breakfast. Fifty people have gathered to see the start of the regatta, but she is not one of them.

Tom spots Phil's wife in the crowd, smiling and waving. She blows Phil a good luck kiss.

African air. It is like no other in the world. To smell it, to breathe it that first time, is less like an involuntary action, an unconscious sense, and more like an experience, a life-altering event. Tom's perhaps a bit dramatic about it, a little too precious, but he doesn't care.

It has little to do with the climate, the heat and humidity, the strangeness of the local food and the flavour of sweat it produces from its people. You can experience that almost anywhere, from Bangkok to Beijing, Bali to Boracay, as well as the traffic, the pollution, and the dodgy sanitation. African air is richer than that. The true African scent is of the earth itself, all that is pure and natural and alive. Mostly it is the smell of animals, wild animals – the great cattle-yard hum of a thousand grazing wildebeest on the savannah. Then there's the moment before an afternoon rainstorm, clouds gathering on the horizon, swollen and black as bruises and cracking like a sweat to cool the bleached grass of the plain, the baked ground, the dry riverbeds. And lush, wooded valleys, mountains, greener than you ever thought Africa to be, sweet-scented and heavy with the fruit of the wet season.

But like any first experience, any life-altering event, it fades. It fades and you are never aware of how or when or at what rate it fades. You simply wake up one morning, go about your day, and it's gone. It's still there in the physical sense, but somehow you are insensitive to it. Somehow you have been numbed by overexposure. The air is still the air. You breathe it. You are aware of it. It sustains you. But no matter how hard you try to relive the heady rush of that first immersion, you will never find it again. At least not in the way you did before. Others will find it. There will always be others. They will take the steps you have taken, see the places you have seen, and they will smell the air, breathe it, and will be as moved by it as you were that first time.

But to you it is something experienced, gained, and then lost. Sure, you have the memory of it, perhaps a few hundred photographs, a souvenir, diary entries, or emails written home to console your recollection, but that is all. It becomes history, and like any history, the facts are obscured by distance. Not by miles, but by time.

Tom guesses that's why travellers keep on travelling. A traveller never settles for one country, one continent. Once a path has been beaten, no matter how remote and exotic, the latest glossy brochure can appear an attractive option.

Maybe it's the same with lovers, with husbands and wives.

The run out to the island is slow. No wind. After the cheers, the sprinting down the sand, the push off from the shore, the jumping into the catamarans and the scrambling into positions, it's almost an anticlimax. It's quiet out on the lake. The island is there, a half-submerged tombstone battered and grey and mottled green with moss.

Tom glances to his right to check the progress of the other boats. All three are together, only a few metres apart. He can hear laughter in the distance across the water, a few shouts. Thanks to Phil, they are a long way in front.

So now, with little else to do, except for when Phil tells him to yank on a rope and tighten a sail, Tom sits back and thinks about Kate. He wonders if he really hates her. Hate is a strong word, maybe *too* strong. Maybe it's just a passing thing. They've been through rough patches before and they got through them. But how many rough patches does it take before it just becomes rough? Maybe it's just Africa. Maybe it's just being away from home so long, missing friends, family, pitching a tent forty-seven times, drinking too much, sunburn, dehydration, chronic diarrhoea, and, possibly, the onset of malaria.

It certainly didn't start out that way. A year ago they were united. Kate was pregnant with their first child, into her second term. And just like any other successful young couple, they loved the thought of that baby, their little human being. They'd already decided on a name. Boy or girl, Charlie or Charley, it didn't matter either way. It was a dedication to Kate's father and Tom's grandfather, both Charlies and good men.

Kate said she didn't care about the sex of the baby, and Tom agreed, but sometimes he wished it to be a little girl. Tracing his fingers over Kate's growing belly, he imagined inside a tiny heart, a tiny hand. He couldn't wait to hold that tiny hand, the span no greater than the breadth of his index finger, and hold that hand until it grew into the hand of a woman. Holding that hand, he'd guide and protect her. He'd warn her about boys and about men. He'd keep her safe. He'd keep her from getting broken.

The baby changed Kate's body, but it soon changed her in other ways.

I'm a fucking vessel, she said one night, tossing and turning, unable to sleep.

A what? Tom asked.

A vessel, Kate said. Seven years at university, two degrees, a Masters, and all I've become is a fucking vessel. I'm not a person. I'm not a woman anymore. I've become a transporter of fucking cargo!

You're a woman, Tom told her. Women have babies. That's just the way it is. It's beautiful, Katie. *You're* beautiful.

Beautiful! Kate exploded. You think a fat arse is beautiful? Swollen ankles? What about stretchmarks and gigantic breasts?

Tom laughed. The breasts I like.

Like them do you? Well, you can have them! Have it all, Tom, and see how you fucking like it!

Tom was away on business, at a mining conference in Beijing when Kate lost the baby. She didn't blame him. At least Tom didn't *think* she did. Except for the night he arrived home from the airport and found her on her hands and knees on the bathroom floor scrubbing away the blood, they never talked about the baby again, their little Charley. It was an unspoken promise between them. And they never talked about trying again. Sure, they had sex – albeit less often and lacking a noticeable measure of passion – but they were careful. The pain numbed them. It numbed Kate, anyway.

Kate went back to work soon after. She scored a government job with Child Safety. Tom thought it was too soon but Kate said she was okay. He was confused. He'd expected something else, something a bit more dramatic. Her pain he could handle, her mourning, her grief. He could handle the tears, the sleepless nights, the questions why, the guilt, the loss, the failure, and in a way, he almost welcomed it. But it never came. Not once. Kate just got on with things. She woke in the morning, ate breakfast, dressed and went to work. She got home from work, ate dinner, chatted with friends on the phone, on Facebook, watched a bit of TV and went to bed. And she did it every day and night as though nothing had ever happened.

It was as frustrating for Tom as it was confusing. How could she be so cold? What kind of woman dismisses a miscarriage with such flagrant indifference? Didn't she ever feel that baby was part of her, part of *them*? Did it mean anything, anything at all? Kate's Child Safety job, Tom reasoned, gave her direction, a purpose. But it also gave her a certain distance. She could protect those kids. She could write her reports. She could be compassionate, supportive and professional. She could make a difference in their lives. But at the end of each day Kate never had to bring those kids home. She never had to watch them suffer after five o'clock. She could reduce them to figures, statistics, and file them away.

Africa was Plan B. Let's go to Africa, Tom said. Let's go on safari. And let's do it properly. We'll backpack. We'll camp. We'll do it on the cheap. Let's start in Egypt and work our way down. Cairo to Cape Town. The length of the fucking continent!

Tom said these things, and Kate agreed, but the one thing he didn't say is that he hoped Africa would save them, somehow mend the broken parts.

Tom thought it, and he guessed Kate thought it, but he never said it.

They saved their money. They bought the tickets.

They made it to Africa.

How long have you been married? Tom asks Phil as they round the island.

Almost six years.

Same. Any kids?

Not that I know of, Phil laughs.

And you're happy?

Sure.

Tom glances toward the shore. From this distance the campsite, the people on the beach, the huts and the tents are a diorama, expertly constructed but nothing real.

Do you ever get bored?

Bored? Phil says.

I mean, once you're married, that's *it*.

That's the whole point, isn't it?

Yeah, Tom says, but you must look at other women.

Sure, Phil says. I look. I'm still a man. But it's just *looking*, nothing else. If you're with the right person it doesn't matter.

And how do you know if you're with the right person?

I don't know *how* you know, Phil says. You just *know*.

And do you think your wife feels the same way?

I bloody *hope* so, Phil laughs again. We'd be wasting our time if she didn't!

About fifty metres offshore, Tom knows they have the regatta won. The Brothers are a distant second, having just rounded the island. The Americans and the English lads have conceded, drawn up their catamarans, stripped down out of their lifejackets and board shorts, and are bomb-diving naked from the rocks. The crowd greets them on the shore. They cheer as Tom and Phil share a high five, drag their boat onto the sand and run up the beach toward the bar. They don't need to run. It's more for effect than anything else.

The trophy sits on the bar top, the *Malawi Cup*. Tom orders two Elephant beers and they toast their victory with triumphant smiles and the clinking of bottlenecks. The crowd from the beach pushes in behind them. Sweaty, salty, sandy, and sweetened with coconut oil and mango daiquiris, it wears *Paradise* as if it's duty free bottled cologne.

Someone slaps Tom on the back. It's the English girl, the starter of the regatta, lunging toward him with bare, sun-sharpened breasts. What's her name again?

Phil's wife is there, smiling.

Who gets to keep the trophy? Tom asks.

Six months each is the rule.

But we won't know each other in six months.

No, Phil says, a knowing smile cracking his sunscreen. We probably won't.

It's a good trophy, Tom says.

You keep it, then, Phil says. He grins and wraps an arm around his wife, draws her into his chest. Small and blonde, she purrs. Then he says, after raising his beer and necking half the bottle in an inexpert but spectacular swallow, golden Elephant dripping from his chin, Maybe you can show it to the grandkids someday.

A column of horses enter the far end of camp, amble down the track from the dusty road and gather in a circle on the sand by the shore of the lake. At the bar through the crowd of half-naked bodies, the drooping palm fronds of the hut's roof and the glaring sunshine beating off the sand, Tom picks out Kate as the riders dismount. Proud, half-drunk with beer and victory, he wants to snatch up the trophy from the bar, race shirtless and barefooted across the white-hot sand, take her in his arms, lift her, kiss her, twirl her about and present to her his prize, his glorious and unique *Malawi Cup*. But then, beside her, he notices Joe. They're smiling the same giddy smile and handing the reins of their horses to the guide. The guide smiles back at them, waves, and together they stroll up the beach toward the bar hut.

Joe stops at the bar, orders two mango daiquiris. Tom grunts recognition. Kate walks by only metres away, shouldering through the crowd, heading for a table in the sun. She's gorgeous, this woman, this stranger shimmering hot and wet in a black string bikini. Tom waits with a ready smile, a tender look that he hopes will say, Come here, my darling. Let's not fight. We were fools. Let me hold you. You are beautiful. I love you.

But Kate doesn't look at Tom as she passes. It's like he's not here.

Once Joe is gone, at the table in the sun with Kate and the daiquiris, Tom takes up the trophy from the bar. Alone in the crowd, alone with Phil and his wife pressed against his shoulder, the English girl's erect nipples gouging holes in his back, he turns the *Malawi Cup* in his hands. It really is a good trophy, something to show the people back home. He looks at it, studies each knot and curve, questioning for a moment its hopeful acceptance through customs, and then down at his bare feet dangling from the barstool.

The tops have begun to brown, white between the toes.

Like most things, Tom guesses, the tan will fade.

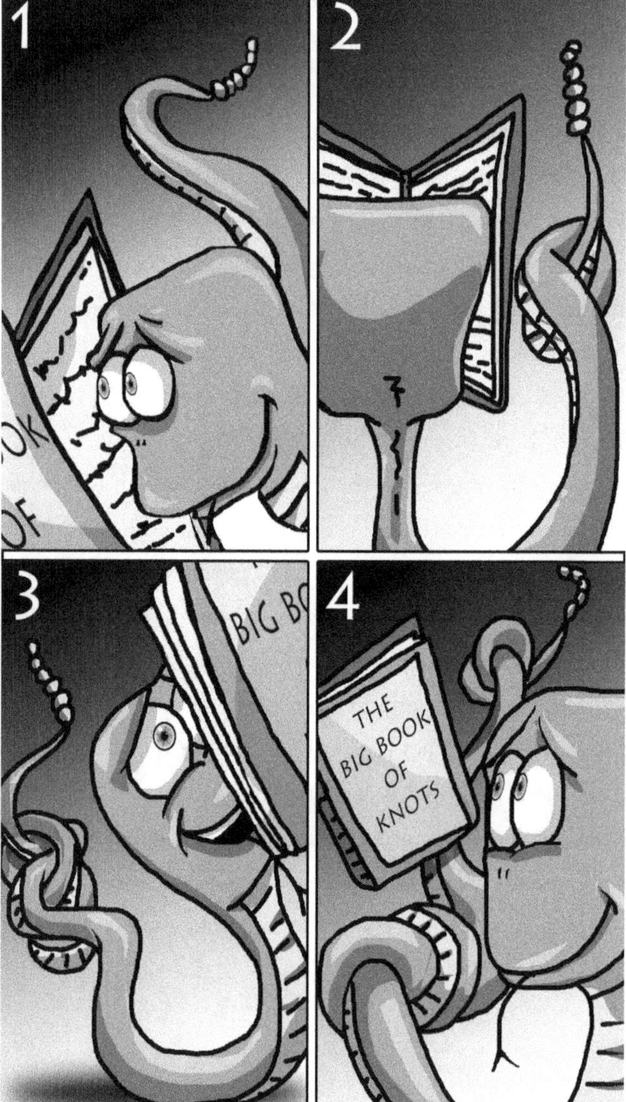
OK
OF
BIG BO
THE
BIG BOOK
OF
KNOTS

Pretty Birds

D. Robert Grixti

White Cockatiel

Thursday, 8 April 2010

Decided today I'm gonna start keeping birds again. It's mainly 'cause Dr Alayna told me to take up a hobby. She says therapy only gives you the tools to help yourself and change how you think of things. Usually she just gives me pills and even though the little paper inside the bottle reckons they work just fine on their own she said if I keep myself busy they'll work even better. I haven't got no job since I was away for so long and I'm always bored and Dr Alayna says when you get restless it's harder to make bad feelings go away.

So, Joe, you told me you used to care for a pet bird. That sounds like a healthy way to occupy your time, she said and she's the doctor so she knows best.

I ain't really the writing type but the doc said it's a good idea to maybe put it all down in a journal like at school when you take notes so you remember stuff for later. The last time I tried to keep birds it didn't end well but this time I'm gonna make sure I do it right.

Friday, 9 April 2010

Today I bought some bricks, timber and chicken wire from the hardware store. If I'm serious about keeping birds then of course I gotta have one of them big aviaries.

What kinda birds you gonna have? asked the guy when I was paying for the things. *Pretty ones*, I told him. *I only like the pretty ones that are nice to look at* and then he said, *Plenty of different birds out there. Just depends on what you're lookin' for.*

Now the reason I wanna keep birds is 'cause I've got an anger problem and recently I've decided to try and work through it. Doc says I gotta start making healthy lifestyle choices 'cause these things are mostly about willpower. It's gonna take a long time to sort this problem out, though. I've had it as long as I can remember and now I'm 37 so I have to be in it for the long haul. If I wanna keep birds for a long time they've gotta be comfortable. They just end up causin' too much trouble otherwise.

Wednesday, 14 April 2010

Aviary's going well but I have to slow down every now and then 'cause my bones aren't what they used to be and hammering or sawing too long tires me out. I've got a good friend, Richie, who told me all about how to keep birds – the correct way to catch 'em and how to build a good aviary to keep 'em locked up safe and sound. He sure knows his stuff. My aviary ain't nowhere finished yet but I can already see it's heaps better than the cage I had when I tried keeping birds last time – much safer and more secure.

Last time I did this I tried keeping a beautiful white bird with a red head and a pretty tail that wiggled from left to right. She was easy to catch 'cause she hadn't been out of the nest for long and she ventured off far away from the other birds. I didn't know how to set up a good aviary then so she wasn't happy in her cage, which was too small and she kept on making a fuss to be let out. The old bitch who lived upstairs heard all the noise and reported it and then I had to let my bird go free.

Everyone said it was cruel to cage up a wild bird without tryin' to tame it first. It was stupid too, 'cause the noise gets you in trouble with the neighbours.

That's when I had to go away for a long time, and there I met Richie and I learned so much and now I reckon I could keep birds properly.

Saturday, 17 April 2010

Finished building my aviary today, so now I need to set my mind to looking for a bird to put in it.

Richie reckons it's our duty to nature to keep watch over birds. They're fickle creatures and it's a waste when the pretty ones flit around everywhere and get into trouble. Lots of 'em are endangered and that's why it's a good thing to keep 'em in captivity like they do in the zoo. It's a nice warm relaxing thing, the feeling of sticky sweetness I get from taking care of 'em. Most people don't care for keeping birds but I'm happy to do it 'cause they're such pretty things and it's what's good for 'em in the long run.

I built my aviary in the basement where there's lots of room and it's quiet and out of the way and the neighbours won't hear anything. There's a tiny window in the basement where only a little bit of sun comes in each day. It's important for 'em to have a little sunlight but not too much. Just enough so they don't forget the sun exists but not enough to overexcite 'em. Richie says birds are easier to manage in the dark 'cause it subdues 'em and they take to their cages a lot better.

Thursday, 29 April 2010

Today I had my appointment with Dr Alayna and she asked me, *What type of bird are you planning on getting, Joe?* and then I said I didn't know and I asked her what kinda birds she likes and she said she likes the ones that talk back to you and I said I don't like birds that talk a lot but I like the pretty ones and she said, *Well, there are plenty of birds you can keep as pets that don't talk* and told me all I've gotta do is look around until I find one I want.

Tomorrow I will start looking. It has to be a bird I like otherwise there isn't any point. Dr Alayna always says if I don't see a point then I'm not working on my problem.

Wild Canary

Sunday, 2 May 2010

Found a pretty bird today on the trail which runs by the creek outside the yard. She is a little timid one with a lithe body and thick yellow plumage all over. I was walking along under the trees and I saw her and I thought it would be nice to have such a pretty bird so I reached out and snatched her and she gave a little screech but I coaxed her to sleep warm in my hands and then she was a lot calmer.

The thing about birds, my friend Richie says, is they settle down quicker if you get 'em used to you first. So I sat in the cage with her until she woke up and stroked her and whispered, *It's okay, bird, it's okay. I ain't gonna hurt you* and tried to play with her to make her be at ease.

I don't think she's quite settled in yet 'cause she scratched my hand and it bled and I needed a Band-Aid and so I yelled at her and forced her to stay in her nest in the corner so she could have a time-out. Sometimes birds can be aggressive if they don't know you and you have to make sure they know it's not acceptable behaviour.

Wednesday, 12 May 2010

My bird is still not settled in the aviary. The other day when I left her food in the cage she came at me and startled me and tried to get out the door. She has been in the wild for a long time and is not used to being in a cage. She is restless but I think she is starting to adjust to her new home. All I have to do is grab her and hold her tight and then she calms down again and I can put her in her nest and she will stay there. She will learn to stay put pretty soon.

Maybe if she is good by the end of this week I will let her out for a bit of fresh air. It should be okay if she is calmer by then; I will just stay outside with her. Richie says birds are flighty when you give 'em freedom but if you keep a close eye on 'em they know they always have to come back. He always said he knew *everything* about birds and he knew the best ways to keep 'em in line 'cause he's had a lot of birds and sometimes they'd cause trouble.

Thursday, 13 May 2010

Richie's bird care tips (that I can remember)

1. Give 'em lots of treats 'cause it keeps 'em happy and they like the attention.
2. When they get snippy make sure you punish 'em or they think they can do it again and again.

3.   Let 'em out sometimes so they don't get stir crazy but not too much.

4.   Get 'em used to being handled nice and early so they don't try to fight you when you touch 'em.

Monday, 17 May 2010

Feeling a little sad today 'cause my new bird still has not taken to me. When I went to let her out for a while today she screeched and attacked me and made a nasty scratch on my forearm, which I cleaned with rubbing alcohol (and that hurts).

I called up Richie and he said she was too aggressive and there was nothing I could do about it, so I decided to get rid of her.

I wrapped her up in a blanket and took her back out to the trail where I found her and I left her there under one of the trees for the other birds to find. She was such a pretty bird and it seemed like a waste to get rid of her but some birds are like that and are just frigid and won't take to you no matter what you do.

I have cleaned out the aviary so it's ready for a new bird. I will try to get a more docile bird this time.

Common Barn Owl

Thursday, 20 May 2010

Dr Alayna asked me how my bird keeping was going and

I said I'd gotten rid of my bird but I'm getting a new one soon 'cause I've been a lot calmer and more focused having one. I told her I still felt the warm, sticky sweet feeling 'cause I take care of birds even when they are frigid ones but a calmer bird will be easier for me and a lot less strain.

She smiled at me and said it's good I've found a way to work through my problem and that I'm sticking with it 'cause there is still a long way to go. Dr Alayna has a very pretty smile.

She reckons my anger problem might have developed in high school. She says I'm frustrated 'cause when you're a teenager you create an identity by talking with other people and I did not do that. I ain't never been good with other people. In high school, everybody said I was creepy and weird, and I probably *was* weird – 'cause my mum would always yell at me and say I'm not normal. Even now as a grown up I am still not good with people but at least I can still keep birds 'cause the birds need me to take care of 'em and I feel good about myself and best of all I don't need to talk to 'em.

Friday, 28 May 2010
I think I will try and get a nocturnal bird. My friend Richie says they're docile during the day and it is easier to catch 'em 'cause you can sneak up on 'em in the dark.

All of the birds he has had in the past have been nocturnal birds. He said they are just as pretty as any other bird when you look at 'em in the daylight.

Saturday, 5 June 2010

I got a nocturnal bird like Richie said and she is resting now inside the aviary. He is right about them being pretty and she is a handsome brown coloured bird with wide green eyes and a voluminous chest full of plumage pleasing to the touch.

As soon as I got her in the cage I wrapped her in a blanket and gave her a drink and she didn't complain and soon she was fast asleep and so I laid her down right there in her nest and took care of her and I got it done much quicker and easier than with the last bird.

So far she hasn't tried to get away even once and I know she won't 'cause her cage is set up in the basement where it is dark all day and nocturnal birds are at home in the darkness and she'll be calm and happy in her nest.

Sunday, 6 June 2010

Spent all day taking care of the nocturnal bird. It's nice sitting in the aviary with her and stroking her 'cause I know she won't try to get away so long as I'm there when she wakes up to feed and water her and after that she settles back down in her nest and dozes off.

Richie came over to see her too and he said she is the easiest bird he has ever seen. I let him in the aviary and we sat there together, enjoying the bird's company. He said to me, *Some people out there have a lotta trouble with birds, Joe, but not us. We don't have no trouble with 'em at all.*

Later on he said I've inspired him to start keepin' birds again. Maybe I can help him set his aviary up and pick some pretty birds out for him. I reckon he'd like that.

Tuesday, 8 June 2010

The nocturnal bird drinks so much, it's a wonder she doesn't swell up like a water balloon and pop and fill the basement with water. All she does is drink and sleep and even when she's awake she just sits perched in her nest staring at me with her green eyes, moaning softly in protest until I take care of her again.

I borrowed one of those camp beds that you blow up from Richie and set it up in the basement next to the aviary. Although the bird is docile most of the time, she is most docile during the night 'cause the darkness calms her down and I don't need to give her drinks anymore and it's the best time to take care of her. I'm sleeping down here now – so I can be here when she needs me and be ready to take care of her at a moment's notice.

Friday, 11 June 2010

Something horrible happened today. I woke up to find the nocturnal bird dead on the bottom of the cage. I'm very shocked 'cause she was perfectly fine last night and I don't know what happened. Richie came over and checked her and he said he thinks maybe I gave her too much to drink. *You can't give 'em too much of that shit, Joe. It clogs up their system and then they can't breathe no more.*

He helped me take her down to the river to the place I got rid of the last bird and we gave her a proper grave. He told me I shouldn't keep birds anymore but I can't agree – I have to work through my problem like Dr Alayna said. I can't stop now.

~~Wednesday, June 16 2010~~
~~Can't help but wonder maybe Richie was~~
Nah, don't worry about it.

Mourning Dove

Thursday, 17 June 2010

Couldn't get the dead bird out of my mind so I told Dr Alayna about it since her job's to make me feel better. She went pale and told me she couldn't help me anymore and that my problem's gotten much worse. *You're sick, Joe,* she said. *You're really,* really *sick, Joe.* Well, I figure, if I'm still sick then she's not so good at her job after all. It's up to me to make myself feel better on my own.

So now I haven't got any more appointments with Dr Alayna. But I'm not giving up on my bird keeping. I've already got a new bird to take care of and she is the prettiest one yet. I can't wait to start taking care of her. I hope I'll get to make her smile.

She has a very pretty smile.

Tilly

Mal McClenaghan

'I could have been a Jesus freak, but I became an alcoholic instead.'

Excuse me?

What the actual fuck?

I should, I guess, thank someone that I'm not yet thirty and have already heard the worst pick-up line ever.

Check self for excess cleavage, unbuttoned shirt buttons or skirt tucked into my undies – anything that could possibly have earned me this attention. I'm okay, so he's the weird one. Always wise to double check.

'Excuse me?'

Shit, no. Rule One when dealing with losers is to never answer them. *Never.* I stop at my favourite bar for a quiet drink on the way home after a crap day pandering to the needs of the company MD (Mental Defective), and meet another one – this one a self-confessed soak. Pat yourself on the back. Lucky Tilly. Jackpot. Three cherries. Must be my lucky day. I should buy a lottery ticket.

Or capsicum spray. I'm thinking maybe the capsicum spray.

'No,' says the soak, slowly. 'Not you, the guy behind you.'

The bar is empty except for the soak, the geriatric barman with the gruff one word vocabulary ('kanidoforya'), and me.

Great. Even if Soaky the soak is seeing double, apparently, I'm now a guy. So much for being hit on. Way to make a girl feel special.

Soaky offers his hand. Thinks about speaking for a second and then ditches the idea.

My hand doesn't move from my bag where it should now be closing around the capsicum spray I bought instead of a lottery ticket.

'You didn't see him, did ya? Well ...' Soaky drains his glass. 'Well, he sees you an' he wants to talk. To you.'

'So, an invisible man behind me wants to talk? What does he want to talk about?'

Sorry. Sarcasm has always been my second language. Snarky Tilly.

'He just wants to say sorry. He wants to say that it wasn' your fault.' Soaky looks fairly convincingly over my shoulder. 'Isn' that right, Jacob?'

No.

No, no, no.

Fucking no.

The feeling of being profoundly afraid and failing to comprehend why, that's what I have. The feeling your bowels are filled with ice water. I have that one too.

'Not funny, Soaky.'

Jacob is gone forever, I know that. The fucking coward walked. I down the last of my drink. But I don't turn, and I don't walk. Soaky slides his glass over to me.

'Mine's a Jack. You wanna talk to Jacob?'

Do I want to talk to Jacob?

I want to punch Jacob. Slap his face. Beat my fists against his chest.

Hey, I'm all over the steps of grieving. I've done fear and denial and anger and more anger and more fucking anger. I stopped there though. I stopped at fucking anger because it worked. Anger at his family blaming me. Anger at him leaving.

On our honeymoon.

Of course I wanted to talk. I wanted to tell him what an arse he was.

'I lost my wife a couple of years ago.' Soaky taps his glass. 'To this.'

Soaky's story has a price. I buy refills.

Talk to Jacob. Okay, I can do that.

'I wanted to talk to Julie after she was gone; I was so lonely. I knew she was there, I could, y'know, feel it.' Soaky waves his fingertips in the classic children's *Booga-Booga* fashion. 'So I listened, and you know, in the quiet for Julie. The quiet under the static of people talking about their workday and what kind of fuckin' BMW the company should buy them …'

'And the barking dogs and the traffic noise and the—'

'Ex-actly!' Soaky is triumphant. 'Under all that stuff is a buzz in your head like, like a …' Soaky flaps his outstretched arms in slow motion. Particular attention is paid to the Javanese-dancer cock of the wrist.

'Pterodactyl?' I offer.

'Naw, a thing …'

'Gargoyle?'

'A fuckin …' Two more flaps. '… Butterfly!' Cue priceless wide-mouthed grin from Soaky.

Well, we finally got there.

'So, let me get this. Under all the day's white noise is a butterfly that is Julie in your head wanting to talk with you.'

'No! You're makin' fun of it.'

Scowl. Cue grumpy Soaky.

Grumpy Soaky won't finish the story. Grumpy Soaky wraps his hand around the empty Jack glass and won't meet my eyes.

I remember the unspoken secret language of the serious and attentive listener. I buy Soaky a double.

'So,' he goes on, after dribbling in the double, 'un-der the big noise is a little noise and in-side the little noise is Jacob.' He drains the rest of the shot. 'Or Julie. Or someone else. Sometime lots of someone-elseses.'

Elseses?

Soaky puts his chin down on the table.

'I've fuckin' talked to Jesus.' He looks up without moving his chin from the table. 'Almost makes you a believer, right?'

Umm. Let me think about that. No, it doesn't.

It's comical, watching the top of Soaky's head move when he speaks, but I need to go. I have work in the morning. I have responsibilities and a life to get on with.

Why do I bullshit myself?

'I'm going. Need a lift somewhere?'

'No, no. Michael will take me home if I get drunk.'

He waves a hand towards Mr Congeniality, the barman, who neither smiles nor acknowledges Soaky's wave.

If I get drunk. Hmm.

'Here, taxi-fare.'

I tuck thirty dollars into the pocket of Soaky's flannel shirt. The moist pocket of Soaky's flannel shirt.

'Bye.'

Soaky gives me a wave. Or maybe it's early Parkinson's. I leave and feel sorry for him; I can see Michael continuing to fill his glass until Soaky's wallet, and taxi-fare, are gone, and then Michael will set him out on the street to sober up.

This isn't a premonition. My father was an alcoholic.

I vow I'm going to follow Soaky's advice, bought as it was with, let me think, seven shots of Jack and a $30 taxi-fare. Cheap though, if it works.

Cheaper than therapy.

Cheaper than going insane.

I'll try it tomorrow. Or on the weekend, when the neighbours play *ABBA's Greatest Hits* and try to pretend they are twenty-somethings, not twenty-plus-kilos-to-lose-before-summerthings.

But I don't. I try it now. Right now, in the car. Impatient Tilly.

Come to me, Jacob. We need to talk.

Nothing.

Cars starting. Noisy drunks leaving bars. The guttural grunts of an, I imagine, near-toothless, closely-related couple having noisy, clumsy sex on the bonnet of a battered green Ford in the alleyway.

Mmmm. Young love. It's a wonderful thing to share with the family.

But no Butterfly Ball for Tilly.

Booga-Booga?

Nada.

I drive home listening to Dylan, but that's way too comforting. I change the CD for Joy Division's 'Love Will Tear Us Apart' instead.

Fuck you, Jacob.

Fuck. You.

I try again as I lie in bed. Insomniac Tilly. Hot nights do not a happy girl make.

Under the expletives of the fighting neighbours next door. Under the late night movie blaring from Mr Wanker's home theatre system across the street. Maybe … maybe there's something.

I decide it's the ceiling fan and shut it off.

But it's still there. A hum, not a buzz. Certainly not the sound of Soaky's butterfly. Something in my head says 'water' and I run a bath.

Deep, cool. The water in my ears cuts back the sounds of the street and I wait. And wait.

And wait.

There's something. Under the piles of washing-up in the kitchen. Under the dog-shit strewn around the yard. Under the unpaid bills and messages from debt collectors. Under the letters from solicitors detailing everyone's claim to my husband's estate.

Under it all is a hum: soft, and strangely anharmonic.

It's blue and tastes of salt.

I decide it's the ocean and let it wash over me. I lie at the bottom of the bath, eyes open, staring through water at the dancing shards of dirty-yellow light from the bathroom's bare light-bulb.

Nothing.

This isn't the ocean; it's cold water in a rust-stained enamel tub in a two-bit flophouse that I call home. I pull the plug and sit, knees drawn up against my chest, listening to the hum. Maybe it's Jacob. Maybe it's tinnitus.

Maybe I'm just bullshitting myself again.

I dress without drying; the midsummer night heat will do that soon enough. A black Ramones tee (Jacob's) and a pair of dirty pink shorts. I feel like crap but convince myself that I look like a liquorice allsort. Suitable attire for another attempt. Jacob was fond of liquorice.

And the Ramones.

And, I had thought, me.

Prick.

The beach is close enough for a walk, but I choose to drive. Slack Tilly. I pardon my own lack of energy and blame it on the heat and the booze, but it's emotional lethargy. Poets call it 'ennui'. I call it 'my life turned to shit'.

Even at three-something in the morning there are cars at the pier. Cars filled with young couples starting out on the adventure that is romance. That wonderful, surprising, enthralling rollercoaster come train-wreck that defines their lives until they crash and burn and the next big thing comes along.

Or not. Maybe it's just teens learning to fuck and they've put their hearts in the glove box with the condoms. Good thinking, kids. Keep it up.

Punny Tilly.

The walk to the water is short and the plan is simple:

swim out until it's quiet and float until I hear the hum. Drowning is another possibility, of course, and there's a certain circularity in that. Boy meets girl. Boy and girl fall in love. Boy and girl get married. Boy and girl argue. Boy goes for late night swim and never comes back. Girl goes for a swim and drowns.

Like Romeo and Juliet.

Romeo and Juliet meet the Pacific Ocean.

At least it's the same ocean, right? That has to count for something.

The tide is receding and the swim out is easy. Slow, lazy breaststroke – just the way Jacob liked it. The beach is a blurred memory, the water tugs against my body and I float on my back to meet my man.

Or my maker.

Maybe both.

It's quiet. Just the hum, and me …

… and Jacob.

Jacob.

My. Jacob.

My beautiful Jacob – tall and tough and tanned and not looking at all like someone who had their head dashed, repeatedly, against the pristine coral of the North-east coast.

'Hey, kid. I've missed you.'

The hate, my hate, is gone, scoured away by the face of the man I was going to spend the rest of my life with.

The man I adored.

I want him back. More than anything, I just want him back.

Shit, I want to hold him. To rest my face against his shoulder and cry; cry until I'm tired and empty and weak and I just can't cry any more.

And so I do.

Jacob tells me about his mistake. Jacob tells me about his bad decision. Jacob tells me about his inability to deal with a simple argument between us.

Jacob realises he fucked up badly, both his life and mine.

The sound of the hum changes, rises, becomes more discordant and I hit the snooze button on the alarm. I don't remember driving home, but that's nothing new.

That was six weeks ago, when Jacob and I made peace together.

I've seen him since then. Seen and spoken to him. I didn't even have to follow the hum; he came to me.

I've seen his father, too. And my best friend from high-school who died of an overdose at uni.

And my grandmother.

But mostly now it's just strangers. Lots and lots of strangers.

My people seem to have moved on.

I sit in my favourite cafe and watch children with tubes in their arms and noses tug, without acknowledgement, at their mother's skirts.

I go to the beach at sunset and watch the swimmers, sorry, drowners, with their futile attempts to push back through the waves.

I buy another bottle of Jack and take two, maybe three long pulls from the bottle before I even get to the car park.

It's 9.20 and I'm running late for work, again. Unpunctual Tilly.

But it could be worse.

I could have become a Jesus freak.

The Crying Space

Peter Farrar

Bryce took a step away from his bed and paused where he used to stand. He imagined the carpet dented there, as if heavy furniture had stood for a long time. The marks would be shaped to his feet – slightly pigeon-toed and in front of the window from where he once looked out. He pictured the dusty glass – pockmarked with long gone flurries of rain – which he used to gaze through at the front garden.

Bryce wanted to peer out past the fence. He wanted to see joggers trailing churning breaths as they thumped past. He longed to turn and see his wife's ruffled hair knotted and strewn over the pillow, the vast walls with hanging pictures too small for them, a half-finished book by the bed.

Last night Bec read to him, each word like a fingertip on his face. Somewhere in her reading he nodded off. During the night he woke against the bunched edge of the pillow, then, later, along a dip in their mattress. Last week he said that dip felt as if he was sleeping in a dry creek bed, the uneven springs like angled stones.

Bryce imagined dragging himself up in the morning, to five-day working weeks and coming home to television, to dozing off before the first ad break. He missed seeing the muted colours of his room, yesterday's limp clothes draped over the back of a chair, rows of letters on spines of books, the no spill straw standing from his cup of water.

Dreams cheated him into thinking he *could* still see. He dreamed of dawdling walks through his garden. Flowers drooped heavily with dew and mangled lines of beans and tomatoes stood half dead at the end of their season. At times, wrapped in a billowing coat, he strolled grey laneways with espresso machines hissing from cafes. The sheer joy of those moments brought him awake occasionally, feet jerking through the next step he was to take. Then there were the dreams he wanted to leach out of himself. In those he stood at checkpoints, squinting into the glaring distance at slowly approaching cars; his gun trained on windscreens; his breath shallow as he waited.

'We'll have tests done.' Weeks ago a doctor said that. Bryce had heard a pen picked up. Heard the doctor's chair tilt and sag as he shifted. Even listened to him write. Can you read by listening to handwriting? Was that the pen sweeping side to side to write an *s*?

Something clicked next to Bryce's face. He waited, guessing. Was it a pen? A surgical instrument? He sensed the slow passing of the specialist's hand across his face, only then deciding it must be a torch.

'Can't say what's wrong exactly,' the doctor said. 'No obvious external signs. No sign of a tumour or cyst. Even the tiniest fibers penetrating behind eyes would leave minute scratches.' Again Bryce sensed the torch passing over eyes, peering into them: light sharp and brilliant like the arc of an eclipse. 'Very unusual,' the doctor added.

Bryce had been able to see during the evacuation. Six of them were airlifted. Their Black Hawk helicopter skimmed above sand dunes. The pilot half turned, shouting – above the sound of the rotor – that they were seeing what the end of the world would look like. They watched sand dunes sliding past as the helicopter thudded towards the base. Dust storms had almost buried abandoned cars and ruined walls of houses, as if the weather was trying to wipe away all the tragedy. His eyes worked long enough to last through the debrief. Where did the firing first come from? Which house did you see activity in? How was confirmation to engage given? At what time did you enter the house? Who first rendered assistance to the wounded children?

Bec drove him home from the doctor. Bryce felt her hand straying from the steering wheel to touch his knee. He pictured her tears beading, smudging the broken lines marking lanes. He knew the streets they drove: plane trees, three quarters bare, lining the road; leaves like damped rags dragging along in the wake of passing trams; chairs grouped outside cafes.

Next to Bryce, Bec slept. She breathed slowly, rustling when she turned over. He touched her. Had she lost weight? She was warm under his hands. Had that muscle in her upper arm softened? He lay against her so he felt the length of her down one side. Her breaths and trembles moved through his skin.

Bryce's clothes were left out so he could find them easily in the morning. He fumbled his way out of bed, feeling around obstacles. He felt Bec vault off the bed and hurry to him.

'It's okay,' he chanted softly.

He brushed her bare skin, warmth lifting off her like steam after a shower. He sensed her fear, now as much a part of her as humour, caring, the want to have a baby, buy a bigger house, wear high heels and love of his thumbs kneading into the dips of her shoulders.

Bryce asked Bec to pass his clothes so he could dress. A few minutes later he told her to go ahead and he would follow her to the kitchen. He knew the way, right down to the angle of every step. Bryce was often content to trail Bec, listening to her slow steps and putting his feet where hers landed, as if fitting them into her footprints on the beach. Carefully he edged down the hall. He walked so closely to her he smelt soap on her skin.

'Little more to the left,' Bec said, but Bryce signalled her to silence. He pushed on, drawing back from a corner, sensing it there. Then five steps later he bumped a door.

'Shit!' he said.

Bryce stopped, rigid in mid stride, feeling Bec's hand cupping his arm, steadying him. Then he twisted away, taking clumsy steps until he arrived in the kitchen with its onion and curry sauce smells.

Bryce faced the direction of a chair scraping out from the table. He felt Bec guide him down to it. He sat tilted over the table. He listened to Bec make coffee, cocking his ear to her movements. A spoon rang when she stirred. The mug was set down in front of him. Her fingers closed warmly around his hand, guiding him towards the cup. A telephone rang in the next room. Her footsteps skittered away.

Bryce listened to her speak. Her voice was higher than usual, as if nervous.

'It's the doctor!' she called across the room. 'I'll put him on speaker.'

Bryce swung the chair towards her.

'Bryce can hear you,' she said.

'We've concluded our tests,' the eye specialist said. It caught Bryce out. The doctor's uninterested drawl – how cold it was; car windows being iced up in the morning; frost burning plants – had lulled him into thinking it would be a nothing conversation. Bryce covered his mouth with hand warmed by the coffee mug.

'We think it might be a psychological problem. Eyesight could have shut down because of something horrible that was seen or experienced. It is a condition we know little about. It has occasionally been found in refugees after long journeys. Cambodian boat people, for example. I'd like you both to see a psychologist who works in this field,' he said.

Bryce heard Bec rummaging for a pen and taking down details.

Later, Bryce glided his fingers over the tabletop as if reading Braille. He touched over crumbs, spills and coffee circles. His face lifted up to her as she came closer to him. His eyes followed her movements as if he watched her.

'I'm never going to see again, am I?' he said quietly.

'One day you will. I'm sure of it,' Bec said.

Recently, he had said that now he was unable to pick a lie by seeing her he could take her wrist in his hands to do so. He could tell from her pulse. Whether it would beat ferociously like raindrops fracturing on a window. Bryce knew she stood in front of him then, thin wrists extended towards him, waiting for him to take them. Instead he slowly reached up, finding her rows of knuckles, lines of veins and tapering fingers, until he slipped his hands inside hers. Bec swung her head down to his, kissing him so passionately she forced his head back.

Bryce used to fear going on the patrols and leaving the safety of the base. They drove down narrow roads – considered clear the day before, but by morning they carried the risk someone had planted a mine during the night. Once they found the remains of a missing journalist. One of his shoes lay well off the road. No one wanted to retrieve it in case there was a trap.

Last week Bec drove him to places they used to visit. Bryce knew where they were by how sharply the car cornered, the smell of fish and chips sweeping by, the long wait at a set of lights and clinking of yacht masts. They drove with windows down. Sea air blustered into the car. It vibrated and howled. Bec took him out to the pier he used to fish from. Bryce listened to the water. Ribbed with small waves, the sea foamed and slopped into the wooden pier. Bec asked him to talk about fishing there in minute detail: catching a flounder, its body as narrow as flowers pressed in a book; the rush of line across fingers; the slow days when there was nothing but the smell of bait in the sun and tourists asking if anything bit around here besides teenagers on each other's necks. Bryce knew what she was trying to do; trying to bring his eyes back to life, using smells and recollections while talking quietly to him.

'Here,' Bec said, so close her breath layered over his ear. Bryce imagined touching his skin there, feeling the soft edges of her words brushing him. Bryce smelt toast as Bec pushed a plate towards him. He found his way to the jam and vegemite. His hands knew the shape of the jars. At times he smelt the contents. Bryce noticed smells more often now. 'Tree Dahlias,' he said yesterday and there they were: lilac petals feathering over ground.

Bryce could not help with directions anymore. He was unable to tell her to turn left here, or that there was a parking spot ahead. Soon they arrived in another waiting room. Bec commented that there were French impressionist prints. Old magazines with crosswords finished and recipes torn out. They sat. Cars wisped by outside. Bryce smelt perfume, probably from the receptionist, the vapor burning inside his nostrils.

'What was the last thing you remember seeing prior to the blindness?' the psychologist asked once they were seated in the office. 'Tell me about the seventy-two or so hours before. Was there anything especially traumatic that happened leading up to losing your sight?'

Anything especially traumatic? Bryce could have laughed. How about that child so burnt her skin was leathery black? Would you settle for the taxi driver they shot dead carrying nothing more than cash and a picture of his wife? What about that bomb detonated in the market that Bryce couldn't stop replaying through his mind?

The psychologist wrote everything down. The pauses between questions dragged out. Finally, he told them he would be in touch. The psychologist said he understood it was difficult. They may well not be looking at an operation or medicine.

Afterwards Bec took Bryce for coffee. He listened to her wrap his latte in a serviette. He told her it was hopeless. Maybe he should count his blessings that he came home with arms and legs, or that he was not on a kidney recipient list because of shrapnel wounds. He heard her turn in the chair. From her breathing he could tell she was facing away. Probably facing rows of shop windows where the layered reflections of passing people glided by.

When they went home Bryce knew what Bec would do. She often hurried to a small space behind the shed. It was a narrow shaded area, damp and overgrown by clover. Bec once told him it was her crying space. She said it was where sobs came up lumpy and hard. Between creeper dangling down from the shed and the splintering fence she recovered and found strength, steadying herself and finally retracing steps to the house. Bryce sometimes picked the difference in her voice when she returned inside. It croaked and broke. Bryce concentrated on her. He had picked the difference in how she walked, her skidding hurried steps when she was trying to keep herself busy, her heavy, pausing steps when she was preoccupied.

They finished their coffee in silence.

Bryce had called out from his bunk at the base. Somewhere between confused dreams of running, crouching and taking cover pressed into the walls of shattered houses. When he cried out his voice echoed back to him, pinging between beds, floors and walls. 'Can't see! Can't see!' he shouted over and over, until rushing steps crowded around him. Someone told him to calm down; another asked what happened. Bryce sat up, blinking, wiping the heels of his palms through his eyes. Within an hour he was lying on a stretcher in a helicopter, feeling a draught as heavy as bad breath cutting across his face. Someone whose voice he had never heard before kept reassuring him.

In the afternoon Bec read again to Bryce. He sat rigidly. Lately he noticed her use her voice differently, letting it lift and fall, depending on which character's lines she spoke. During her pauses he wondered if there was more to her words than the characters she brought to life, that there was also the texture of her own pain. Eventually Bryce slumped, dozing. The puff of air from the closing book briefly roused him. He heard Bec stand. Her steps seemed so quiet they were weightless. Only when she eased through the backdoor did he open his eyes. He imagined her crossing the cracked back path, passing stunted roses towards her space. Bryce gave her the moments he knew she needed.

Later, Bryce stood and the chair wobbled under him. He walked unsteadily, arms floating sideways for balance. He approached, step after tentative step, off concrete onto grass, just missing the possum-scratched trunk of the gum tree, a hand brushing the old metal clothesline. He knew where she was in the same way he had learnt to find his way to the sink, to stand in front of music or take her hands.

Bryce heard her say his name quietly. For a second he paused, suspended in the late afternoon cooling sun. He heard Bec leave the space, her next steps coming towards him.

He moved towards her.

Failing To Be

Tess Evans

Ghosts appear in many guises – a flicker of light on a swamp, a shadow on the stair, a whisper on the wind. These we could call the literary ghosts – ghosts of stature, you might say. But there are others – those whose lives and tragedies are small and insignificant. Who glide through the everyday world of factories, lanes and city streets – urban ghosts who jostle and murmur among busy shoppers and weary workers. These are souls who cannot rest in peace.

I know. I am one of them.

In a sense, I always knew I was different, although for a while I played at being one of the living. One of you. It didn't work, of course. It never does. We exist on different planes, you and I. You are made of solid flesh and blood, whereas I … I can only try to explain myself.

I spent my early years with an ailing mother and a busy father, attended to more or less kindly by a series of housekeepers. I was a quiet, serious child, used to being hushed at the slightest noise (*Don't clatter those blocks, child; your mother has a headache*). Often, I was sent outside 'to play', but as I was not allowed to have any friends visit my house, my play consisted of hours sitting in my favourite tree or drawing idly in the dusty earth.

A more robust and resourceful child would have been delighted with this freedom, seeking excitement and adventure with unbridled glee. A more thoughtful child would have read a whole encyclopaedia and a more curious child would have watched the birds and insects and learned their ways. A more creative child would have spent the time building an imaginary kingdom. But me? I just sat and waited to be called in for dinner.

School changed the pattern of my days but I remained aloof from any real engagement with my classmates. I dutifully learned my spelling, chanted my times-tables, played tag with the other children and even ate my lunch with a small group. But if anyone stopped to notice, I rarely spoke and never initiated anything. I did try, in a desultory way, to become a real part of the school community, but this was in the early days and I only succeeded in fading a little more each day.

I can hear you thinking, *Ah, this is someone who will be a victim of schoolyard bullies.* But this was not the case. They simply didn't notice me.

Let me tell you about the games of hide-and-seek I used to play. I would run off and hide like the others. There I'd be, behind a tree, stretched out beside a log or squatting amongst the leaves of one of the many shrubs that bordered the yard of the old country school. The others were found one by one, but no matter how badly hidden I was, no matter how hard I tried to be seen, no-one ever found me. In fact, a new game would start without me being found at all.

In class, I'd be the first to raise my hand to answer a question. But the teachers failed to see or acknowledge me. I was neither a brilliant nor a poor student, and I never misbehaved, so why would they? When teams were picked for various games, I was always one of those few left whom the teacher hastily assigned to a team, so that no-one would have the ignominy of being the 'last pick'. I am only surprised (and I suppose grateful) that the teachers noticed me at all.

I used to look in the mirror night and morning to make sure I was still there, that I hadn't dissolved into air. *A strange child,* you *might* say. *Introspective for one so young.* Others have been less kind, saying I was selfish and self-absorbed. That I imagined slights where there were none.

The death of my mother had very little impact on my life. She was never really there in the sense that other mothers were. She was no more than a presence in a dim-lit room that smelt of lavender and decay.

My father's remarriage to one of the housekeepers could have been my salvation. Peggy was a plump, vivacious young woman, with curly auburn hair and a sweet, china-doll face. She'd been kind to me as a housekeeper and promised that in her new capacity, we'd have lots of wonderful times together. My father was enchanted by her, and together they wove a magic circle of warmth and love in which I was almost, but not quite, included. They did their best, and I don't believe they knew they had failed, but while the child of antagonists may be troubled, the child of lovers is forever excluded.

They took me on picnics, read me stories at night and helped me with my homework. Peggy nursed me through a bad bout of measles and another of chicken pox, but they looked at each other in a way I could never hope to share. Of course I'm not speaking of sex here. It was just that they formed a perfect circle, and although I hovered around the perimeter, they were the circle and I was a separate entity.

I was sixteen when I left home. I heard later that my father and stepmother reported my absence, made some effort to find me and then got on with their lives. What else could they do? Peggy was pregnant, so they wouldn't have missed me for long. Perhaps my little half-brother or sister, a product of that charmed circle, could become part of it more easily than I. I really hope so. I bear no grudges.

No-one noticed me at the railway station (of course). The single train for the day came and went with me on it and that was that.

In the city there are more of my kind.

You don't really see them in the country. (Well, I've been telling you that.) These are the white-faced boys and girls, the needle-scarred prostitutes, the aged men with metho bottles, the shambling old women with their entire world in plastic bags. They are all ghosts, the unseen entities that wander the city streets.

Clichés, you say. *We see them. We simply fail to acknowledge them. Who are they to us? They are not of our species. We all have the power to make our own lives.*

Well, I'm not an educated woman, so I would use clichés, wouldn't I? But some are not yet the ghosts of whom I speak. I'm one of them, although I wear a nice black dress and smart high-heeled shoes.

I work in one of the better department stores, selling ladies lingerie. I'm not without resources, despite what you might think. Upon reaching the city, I spent my meagre savings on one good dress, a fashionable pair of shoes and two weeks' rent in very modest accommodation. Work was reasonably easy to find at that time, and it took only two interviews to secure a position with the respected department store Bailey and Sons Emporium. I was selected, they told me, because I was unassuming, mature and discreet. (*Madam will find the ecru more subtle than the magenta?*) I was good at servility.

My colleagues say good morning and good evening and little else to me. They occasionally cluster and gossip, but this is frowned upon by the floor manager. Despite this, or because of it, I like it here. There is no pressure to belong. I'm just the anonymous sales lady in black. Still, I'm continuing to fade. I feel the light pour through my bones and the image in my mirror is increasingly nebulous.

But today, I made an impact. For a few brief seconds I was solid enough to be seen.

It happened like this. I had a rude customer. Not particularly rude, just demanding – demanding and unseeing. She was beautiful, with luscious ripe breasts, golden skin and a handsome, arrogant face. The sort of woman they say 'turns heads'. She preened in her lacy black bra, smug and confident, totally unaware of the hovering sales assistant.

She only had to look at me. To say something personal. To acknowledge me. But she didn't. She took off the bra, (no modesty) and tossed it in my direction with insolent indifference.

'Get me the red – same size.' I had to bend to pick up the bra. She didn't even bother to look at me when she threw it.

So I killed her.

I don't know why. She was no worse than many others

but I took my professional sales assistant scissors and stabbed her once. Hard. In the throat. She didn't scream. She just looked at me. Really saw me. In that moment my scattering particles coalesced and I was fully and truly there.

No-one else saw me. I wiped my hands (I'm quite fastidious) and left the store. There was blood all over my nice black dress and my high-heeled shoes left rust-coloured footprints, but I walked out unnoticed, melding with the crowd that flows in and around the city streets.

And they all walked past me without a glance. As I speak, I'm moving in and around that commuting crowd, silent and invisible. I've become one of those who cannot rest in peace. For a moment I was real, but now I'm fading faster than ever.

I must find a mirror.

The Broker

Wendy Purcell

'There is nothing so loved that it can't be sold.' Mr Engel nodded sagely. 'Nothing so treasured, nothing with a sentimental attachment so strong, that it can't be severed when the need strikes.

'Take these …' The white-haired old man unlocked a glass sliding door, and pulled out a tray of engagement rings. 'Every one of them a gift of love. You think that all these couples broke up? No, many are still together, still in love, but I have their rings.'

Mr Engel returned the rings to their display case, rolled the glass door back into place on its ball bearing track, and engaged the lock. He straightened up slowly, then leaned forward against the counter. His white cotton shirt strained between the buttons as the weight of his full belly was pushed against the glass. He smiled kindly, his face pulling into a roadmap of wrinkles as he took in the despondent blonde woman on the other side of the counter. Her gaze had barely left the floor. 'It is all right to sell something you love. It is a question of priorities. I understand that. And so should you. There is to be no guilt. What can one do without money in this world?'

The woman smeared a tear over her face with her hand and shook her head. 'Nothing,' she whispered.

'Let me see it then.'

Without speaking, she lifted a black leather case onto the counter.

Mr Engel flicked open the metal catches. Inside, faded blue velvet cradled an old, much polished, brass saxophone.

'I've had it since I was thirteen.' She smiled. 'You should have heard me when I first got it. I think the only reason Dad paid for my lessons was so I'd stop torturing the family with the noises I used to make.' She stroked the neck of the instrument. 'It has a lovely tone.'

'Three hundred and fifty, best I can do.'

Her eyes opened wide. 'It's not enough. Please. I need more than that. Surely it's worth more?'

'I'm sorry, but I can't offer you more. I am being honest with you. It is a student's instrument. You're more than welcome to try somewhere else,' Mr Engel shook his head, 'but you won't do any better.'

She frowned, and then sighed. 'Please, how about at least $500?'

He shook his head.

She turned away, embarrassed.

'Come on, come on.' Mr Engel sidled out from behind the counter and placed a kindly arm about her shoulders. 'What is your name? Nicole? Nicole, things can't be that bad. You come out back with me and I'll make you a cup of tea. You will see, things aren't ever as bad as they seem.' He pushed her in front of him and they parted a beaded curtain with a gentle clatter to enter the back room. Here, in contrast to the crowded front of the shop, the room was sparsely furnished and well-lit.

Mr Engel directed her to a chair, and then filled an old electric porcelain jug with water and switched it on to boil. Light from an overhead fluorescent shone down on his white hair, throwing it into intense relief around the centre of his bald pink scalp. On the back of his fleshy neck, reddened skin folded into crevices so deep they looked like wounds. In all he appeared round, and coloured an alternating series of pink and white – like a worn, faded Christmas ornament.

Mr Engel pulled up a chair at the old table in the middle of the room and sat down with the young woman. 'I can help you, but it will require you selling something you value more than the saxophone.'

'What are you talking about?'

'No, you misunderstand. It is not your body I want, but your memory.' He leant forward, studying her face carefully. 'For the saxophone alone I offer you $350. But for the saxophone and all your memories of it, I offer you $1500.'

'No, no.' She shook her head and made to stand. 'This makes no sense.'

He held out a steadying hand and spoke slowly. 'I will pay you an extra $1150 for your memories of the saxophone. When you got it, how you learned to play it, the songs you have played – in effect, every memory you have that is associated with your saxophone.'

'How can you do that?' Her face had pulled into a frown, but curiosity overrode her fear.

'How is not important. I can assure you it will only take a few seconds and will not cause pain. Actually, you will feel better for it because afterward you will not even remember having had a saxophone. You will have nothing to grieve over, but you will have fifteen hundred dollars.'

'Let me get this straight: you want to buy my memories?'

'I don't want you to leave here unhappy.' He folded his hands together on the table top and sighed before continuing, 'I am a broker; you need money and I can help by purchasing this from you. It is a simple enough transaction. And if I can help another person by later selling your memories to them, then that is a good arrangement, don't you think?'

'I don't know,' she said uncertainly. She looked down at the table, then back up at him out of the corner of her eye. 'If I lose all memory of my saxophone, how will I know you owe me fifteen hundred dollars?'

'I will give it to you before we start.'

'And this won't have any effect on me?'

'None whatsoever. The mind closes instantly over the gaps I leave. It will be as if you never had a saxophone, and that is all.'

'How am I going to explain the fifteen hundred in my purse?'

'A lotto win? Your mind will supply an explanation.'

She gripped the edge of the table. 'And you will give me the fifteen hundred up front?'

'As promised. You agree then?' At her nod Mr Engel got up and went back into the front of shop. The ring of his cash register sounded before the beaded curtain parted again around his portly form. He was carrying the saxophone, and a handful of money. He handed her the cash and then placed the saxophone on the table. 'Give me your hands.'

She reached out to him. He took both hands, turned them palm downwards, and placed them firmly against the cold brass musical instrument. Then he spread his own old, vein-knotted hands over the top of hers and pressed hard. His hands were hot. 'Close your eyes and try to relax,' he told her.

She screwed her eyes tightly shut and tried to take a deep breath. A tingly feeling began behind her forehead. Her eyes flew open.

'You must relax; this will only take a moment. Let

yourself flow with the sensations.' He reached out a hand and closed her eyes.

The tingling started again, rapidly growing stronger.

'Tell me about the day you got the saxophone.' His voice was low and quiet.

'It was my thirteenth birthday. I didn't think I would be getting anything but there … there …' Words fell out of her head. Her mind was strangely blank. What had she been talking about?

'Miss? Miss? Are you alright now?' She looked up. A white-haired old man was handing her a cup of tea. She was in the back of some sort of shop, sitting at a table, and there was a saxophone, or some sort of musical instrument, in front of her. 'Good, you drink this; you will feel better in no time.'

'Where am I? What? I was walking down the street and I …'

'You are safe now. You had a fainting spell outside my shop. But it is alright. You look fine now.'

'I must go.' She stood up and looked around, searching for her handbag. 'I'm sorry to bother you. You've been very kind.' The old man passed across her bag and ushered her through a beaded curtain into a pawn shop. 'Thank you once again. I don't know what could have happened. I'm not given to dizzy spells.' She opened the door, and stepped out into the street.

The door swung to with a soft thud.

Even as a child Jared Lefton had been cruel. His cruelty was not for want of love, as he had been a cherished infant, although his parents' love had gradually dissolved into confusion in the face of his cold unresponsiveness, and later reformed as caution when the viciousness of his character became apparent. He had been an only child for a long time when his younger sister, Emma, had been born, and he had watched with disgust as his father and mother cooed over her. Emma was all tenderness and softness. She was pretty, plump, pink, and useless.

When Jared's parents left Emma alone, Jared would sneak up to the side of her cot. At first she'd eagerly reached out her pudgy hands to him. But then Jared would pinch the flesh of her chubby thighs. She'd screw up her face and scream in protest. The pinching left bruises, but he didn't care. His mother asked him if he knew where the bruises had come from but he had only shrugged in response. Then he started to bring matches into the room. He'd hold Emma's fingers in the flame. She'd screamed so loud he could only do it for a moment before he'd have to stop and pretend that he too had come running in response to her screams. The acrid smell of the extinguished match had tainted the air, and they'd looked at him suspiciously, but he had denied everything.

Soon, Emma began to scream as soon as she saw Jared. He'd had to hold his hand over her mouth to make her shut up. That's when he'd been found out, and sent away.

But now Jared wasn't a child, and he had been done with being sent anywhere. The secret was to find the type of woman who wouldn't scream too loudly, wouldn't run away. Jared pulled a bottle of vermouth from his shopping bag, unscrewed the lid and took a swallow. Take that one, for example. At a bus stop in the street before him were two school children, a boy and a girl, aged about ten. The girl was just asking for it, her short school dress purposely hitched up. Jared inhaled deeply, an erection hardening. He walked to the bus stop and sat down.

'Hello.' He smiled.

'Hello,' the girl returned. The boy didn't respond, his attention entirely taken by his two-thumbed battle with an electronic adversary.

'Would you like to see some baby rabbits?'

'Maybe.' Still only the girl spoke.

'Well, I've got some lovely fluffy little rabbits.' Jared moved closer. He placed his hand on the girl's knee. 'Look, they could sit right here on your lap.'

She clamped her knees together, instantly frightened.

Jared stroked her knee. 'It's okay; don't be nervous. I just want to show you some rabbits.' His thumb circled the soft skin of her thigh. 'Don't you like rabbits?'

'No,' she said firmly, and pushed his hand away.

'Hey!' The boy jumped up, his Nintendo falling to the ground. 'Leave her alone!' He grabbed his backpack and swung it in an arc, hitting Jared over the head.

The girl pulled from Jared's hands and kicked him in the thigh. Then the two children ran off, yelling at the top of their voices.

Jared rubbed his leg. Little bitch. He staggered to his feet. He had to get out of here quickly. The kids had gone into a house and there could be cops any minute. He picked up the boy's electronic game and pocketed it. He might be able to get something for it later.

Jared swore to himself all the way home. Damned little bitch, teasing him like that. Getting around in a short skirt with bare thighs, taunting him. What did she expect? If you're going to hang out the meat you've got to expect to attract flies. They made him sick; they were all sluts anyway. He turned into the gate of his place, kicked some cardboard boxes out of the way and climbed the wooden stairs to his flat.

'Chrissie!' he screamed as he opened the door.

'Jared, is that you?' Chrissie came to the door of the bedroom. She was in her early thirties but looked older. Her hair was too red, her eyeliner smudged. She fingered a wiry lock of hair behind her ear, but it wouldn't stay and sprung forward again in front of her face. 'Where've

you been, love? What have you got? Can I have a drink?'
She'd spotted the bottle of vermouth and held out her
hands. Her fingertips had been decorated with artificial
nails, but now they were chipped and some had pulled
off completely, revealing mangled remnant finger nails
underneath. She smiled her best smile.

'No, fuck off.' Jared shoved her hard and she stumbled
backwards, falling against a chair. Her head struck the
wall with a bang and she slumped to the floor.

Jared nudged her with his foot. She was out cold. He
put the bottle of vermouth on the bedroom chair, then
squatted beside her. He shook her, then slapped her.
Chrissie moaned a little but her eyes remained closed, her
body flaccid.

Jared sat back. He lifted Chrissie's top and looked
at her breasts. Between finger and thumb he took both
nipples and pinched, hard. The erection he'd lost earlier
returned. Eagerly, he pulled Chrissie's pants off and
rolled her over on to her face. He grabbed a pillow off
the bed and shoved it under her hips. Bitch-bitch-bitch.
He gripped her hips tightly, pushing her face deep into
the rug.

Selling things always made Nicholas Engel happier than buying things did. Buying things from people was generally a sad business and Mr Engel didn't like things to be sad. And yet, around his shop were so many sad things: from the ceiling a hundred different musical instruments hung; along the wall TVs and laptops competed for space with microwave ovens and food processors; and in his display cabinets, jewellery, cameras, and military medals lay dull and disowned. All of it was sad; each piece a story of somebody's lost hopes or dreams.

Sometimes though, selling a thing could make a person happier. It could unburden them. We each accumulate possessions, experiences, memories good and bad. Divesting ourselves of things can free us; having something taken away can be a gift. And if the right new owner can be found, the transaction is doubly rewarding, especially to the person who brokered it.

Jared was sitting at the kitchen table. He'd thrown a pack of frozen potato wedges into the oven and was just getting ready to eat when Chrissie staggered in. There was a red lump on her forehead, and one eye was beginning to swell. She raised a bottle to her mouth. Shit, he'd left the vermouth in the bedroom.

Chrissie stood in the doorway and took a swig. 'You're a bastard, Jared.' She waved the bottle at him. 'You think you're a man, but you're nothing.'

He really couldn't be bothered. 'Give me the vermouth, Chrissie.'

'What this?' She took another big swallow.

The bottle was two thirds gone. His bottle. That was it. He lunged for her. She turned to run and the bottle of vermouth flung from her hand, hit the stove and broke. Bitch! He slapped her, then grabbed her by the shoulders and pushed her against the wall.

She yelled in his face, 'I've had enough of you!' He slapped her again and she yelled louder, 'Don't hit me!'

He shook her. 'Shut up!'

'You want me to shut up? You don't want anyone to hear? See what the neighbours think of this!' Her yells changed to, 'He's hitting me! He's hitting me!' She banged the wall behind her with her fists and screamed. 'Help!'

A series of thuds came from upstairs and someone shouted, 'Shut up down there!'

'Help!' Chrissie yelled. 'He's killing me. Help! Call the police!' And she screamed again.

Christ, he did not need this. He shoved her down the hall, grabbed his keys and ran out the door. He kept running down the stairs then out on to the road towards the main street. He kept running til he couldn't hear her anymore. He slowed, then stopped. Leaning forward with his hands on his thighs he tried to catch his breath. Fucking bitch. Another fucking screamer.

He sat back on a fence and tried to think. Jesus what he needed was a drink. If he could get some booze, calm down, he could figure out what to do, but he had no money on him. He pulled a cigarette out to steady his nerves, but his lighter wouldn't catch and he threw it away in frustration. He felt in his pocket for matches or another lighter. Then his fingers found the boy's Nintendo game.

As Jared opened the door to the pawnbroker's shop, Mr Engel looked up and called out a welcoming, 'Hello! How are you today?'

'I'm fine,' Jared muttered. He looked around the crowded shop. So much shit. This fat fucker looked like he'd buy anything. He was sure to get a good price for the Nintendo.

'Is there anything you are particularly after?' Mr Engel asked. He eased his bulk around the counter and came to stand beside Jared.

'I want a hundred for this.' Jared pulled the Nintendo from his pocket.

Mr Engel took the game from him. 'Hmmm,' he

murmured, turning it over. 'It's a little scratched, but it is the advanced version. I'll give you fifty for it.'

'A hundred!'

Mr Engel looked Jared firmly in the eye and repeated slowly, 'Fifty.'

Jared rubbed his face and groaned. God he needed a drink, a cigarette, anything. And he needed to get out of this shit-hole of a shop. 'Alright, fuck it. Fifty then.'

Mr Engel pulled out a grubby fifty-dollar note from his wallet. 'I'll tell you what,' he said, holding the fifty-dollar note just out of Jared's reach. 'I can give you this fifty dollars, or if you have a look around my shop and see something you'd like to buy, you can have anything worth up to seventy dollars.'

'Christ! Just give me my money,' Jared snapped.

'Of course.' Mr Engel calmly handed Jared the note. 'But why not look around anyway? I'm sure you can see something you'd like,' Mr Engel patted him on the shoulder then moved to start dusting an old upright piano. The polished wood veneer of the piano reflected back the eyes of the broker.

Jared stuffed the money in his pocket and made to leave, but just near the door, on the top of an old Singer sewing machine, beside a set of Irish-coffee mugs, in a wooden box filled with costume jewellery, he spotted something grey and sleek.

Jared stopped. What was it? He looked a bit closer. It was a cigarette lighter, fashioned in the shape of a small hand gun. 'Can I look at this?' he asked.

Mr Engel sighed then turned and smiled. 'Let me see now.' He put the duster down and came across the shop. He took the lighter from the box. He peered at it, and then gently tossed it over in his hand. 'Oh yes. Perfect. It is thirty dollars, but I'll give it to you for twenty.'

'Does it work?' Jared asked.

'Of course,' Mr Engel answered. He gave the trigger an experimental click, but no flame appeared. 'I need to fill it up with lighter fluid. I'll fix it for you right now.' He went back behind the counter and through the beaded curtain, leaving it swaying in his wake. He was gone several minutes before returning. He laid the lighter down in front of Jared. 'There, what do you say? '

Jared looked down on it. His eyed widened. He picked it up. It seemed warm, and it felt good in his hand. He pulled the trigger and a flame sprung from the mouth of the gun. He did a quick calculation. If he bought the lighter he'd have thirty dollars left. That'd still get him two bottles of vermouth. 'I'll have it,' he replied.

'Excellent.' Mr Engel beamed at him. 'That'll be twenty dollars.'

Jared handed over his cash without hesitation and pocketed the cigarette lighter.

'I hope you enjoy it,' said the pawnbroker, touching Jared lightly on the hand.

A tingling in the centre of Jared's head pulled him up short. He grabbed hold of a display case until the sensation passed. He shook his head.

'Are you feeling unwell?' The old man was in front of him.

'What's it to you?' Jared snapped back and pushed past the pawnbroker and left the shop.

Jared walked out into the fading daylight. He did not feel right. He needed to get to the bottle shop, but he shuffled undecidedly, not sure which direction to go. The feeling in his head had gone. Only now there was an electric fear prickling under his ribs. He clenched his fists and started to walk further up the main street. His steps grew quicker.

By the time he reached the corner he'd begun to get really scared. The strange feeling was eating away at his insides. He sat on a street bench, breathing heavily, wiping away at the film of cold sweat clinging to his face. He needed to calm down. He clawed in his jacket for a cigarette, pulled one from the box and then retrieved his new lighter from his pants' pocket. He depressed the trigger and the flame sprang into life.

'Come on, Billy, don't hide from Daddy. Daddy loves you.'

Jared started at the voice. He jumped up. 'Who's that? Who's there?' The street had changed, only it wasn't a street anymore. He was inside. There was a desk against a wall and an unmade bed. He saw a school bag lying on the floor beside a deflated soccer ball. He was in a child's bedroom. He could smell an odour like rotten fruit.

'That's it, Billy. You know you have to be good to Daddy.'

Jared looked up nervously as an enormously tall, brown haired man approached him, picked him up and sat him on his lap.

'Put me down!' Jared struggled, but the man was many times bigger than him. Jared screamed.

'No screaming!' the man said and struck Jared hard across the face, knocking him senseless.

When Jared came to, he was lying face down across the bed, held down by an enormous weight: he was pinned, crushed, trapped. There was a terrible pain, a slapping of flesh, someone was moaning. Jared fought to draw breath. On the floor beside him he could see the enormous shadow of the older man rocking backwards and forwards.

Mr Engel picked up the receiver and called for a paramedic. 'Pour soul,' he said. 'He's completely senseless, can't even speak. Yes, that's right, the corner of Main and Bennett. On the bench. You can't miss him. Quite a crowd has gathered.'

Nicole walked briskly down Main Street. She was on her way home with groceries in a bag over one arm, a new cardigan on her shoulders, and new shoes on her feet. Her luck had really changed. She'd won $1500 on a scratchy. $1500! She'd been able to pay her study course fees and buy a few treats. And that one bit of luck had seemed to make more luck happen because now she had a job. A job with a future because now she'd paid her course fees, they had taken her on as an apprentice at *Hair For You*. She couldn't believe how quickly everything could turn around.

She was eager to get home. She'd bought ingredients to make risotto, and a bottle of wine. She had a new flatmate and they were going to have a little celebration in honour of her apprenticeship. She broke into an eager little run, and then tripped up short. She'd kicked off one of her new shoes.

She bent to retrieve it, slipping a finger in at the back and dropping her heel down into the shoe. As she straightened up, her eye was caught by a flash of gold in a shop window. It was a brass saxophone, nestled in a case lined with blue velvet. She looked up. She was in front of a pawnbroker's. She leant towards the window to get a better look, one hand pressed up hard against the glass, little foggy circles forming around each fingertip. The saxophone was beautiful. She had always wanted to learn to play a musical instrument.

On an impulse she opened the shop door and walked in. A round, white haired man greeted her with a broad smile. 'Can I help you?'

'The saxophone,' she said quickly. 'The one in the window. How much is it?'

'Do you know how to play?' he asked.

'No,' she replied. 'But I'd like to learn.'

'Well I'm sure we can work something out. We can always do a payment plan for you.' He moved over to the window display. 'It's a good choice for a beginner.'

Biographies

Gina Boothroyd is a former copywriter of corporate publications, working in-house and freelance. Motherhood put a stop to all that, but the writer within would not shut-up. She has had various articles published in magazines on a range of topics including travel, sport, parenting and autism, and is currently lingering over a novel and a film script.

Laura Bovey is a writer, editor and perpetual student. She lives in Melbourne with her three rambunctious sons and is currently studying a bachelor of Writing & Publishing. This is her second short story to appear in *[untitled]*.

Belinda Campbell lives and writes in the Blue Mountains. Her short stories have appeared in *Southerly*, *Island*, *four W*, *Famous Reporter* and *Flashers*. She is currently working on her first novel, which was 'highly commended' in the 2013 ASA mentorship program.

JM Donellan is an author, slam poet, musician, radio DJ, teacher and voice actor. He has published two novels, *A Beginner's Guide to Dying in India* and *Zeb and the Great Ruckus*. Much more importantly, Margaret Atwood has replied to him on twitter TWO TIMES.

Tess Evans is a Melbourne author who has published poetry, short stories and two novels – *Book Of Lost Threads* and *The Memory Tree*. She began writing in 2006 and before that worked at Northern Melbourne Institute of TAFE.

Peter Farrar was last seen at the Melbourne Writers Festival on his second bottle of shiraz trying to beg everyone looking remotely like a publisher to take his work seriously. He hopes that by the time he submits his next collection of short fiction no one will remember this.

D. Robert Grixti is a speculative and horror fiction author and indie video game developer from Melbourne. His influences, like all aspiring writers of dark fiction, include Stephen King and HP Lovecraft. He writes because he likes telling stories. His debut novel, *Sun Bleached Winter*, was released last December.

Peter Hill has been writing since his first letter to *The Eagle* comic won him fifty pence. Some years later, he moved to New Zealand and became a freelance motoring correspondent, mainly because it allowed him to drive cars he couldn't afford and provided free tickets to motor race events. He continued writing for motoring publications after he moved to Melbourne. More recently, Peter has been writing fiction and has had short stories published in *New Writing, Short and Twisted, 21D*, and *[untitled]*. He completed a Certificate of Professional Writing and Editing. Peter has had a number of technical books published and has a blog on things motoring: http://www.speedsportblog.blogspot.com

Suzannah Marshall Macbeth is a writer and sailor living in Melbourne. She is from Fremantle originally and has a particular interest in writing about place, landscape and the ocean. She has been published in *The Big Issue, Great Circle* and *Voiceworks*. She blogs at equineocean.wordpress. com and you can find her on twitter, @equineocean.

After years channelling Hemingway, **Mal McClenaghan** has decided to channel Ken Bruen instead, writing short shorts in exchange for drinks at the local club. His intention to begin writing children's stories is a cause for concern.

Ryan O'Neill's short stories have appeared in numerous journals and anthologies. His short story collection *The Weight of a Human Heart* (Black Inc) was shortlisted for the 2012 Queensland Literary Awards and the 2012 NSW Premier's Literary Awards. He lives on a property in NSW.

Wendy Purcell lives in Kyneton, Victoria with her husband, three chickens, and two poodles. She loves reading, cooking, a cold gin martini on a warm Friday night, bike riding, beer gardens, and prissy tea parties. This is the first time she has been published.

Adrienne Tam is a Fijian-born Chinese chick with an American accent living in Australia. She is useful at nothing else besides writing stories, which she would happily do for the rest of her life if it actually produced money to pay for food, rent and plane tickets. Still living in hope.

Luke Thomas is a Queensland writer of short fiction. His recent work has appeared in *[untitled]*, *page seventeen*, *Award Winning Australian Writing*, and will feature in the forthcoming edition of *The Sleepers Almanac*. *Home Mechanics*, his short story collection, was shortlisted in the 2012 Queensland Literary Awards for a Manuscript by an Emerging Author. He lives by the beach on the Sunshine Coast.

Venetia Di Pierro is a person who likes doing peopley stuff. She lives with people, talks to people and actually grew two people. She also writes about people. It's school holidays. Her thinking brain is broken. It is full of Lego and children's cries.

KNOWING YOUR AUDIENCE
Thanks for your submission Bob. But the big sellers at the moment are books for teenagers.
Can you condense it down to 160 characters.
Busybird Publi

Also from Busybird

Title: *13 Stories*

Authors: Emilie Collyer, Laurie Steed, George Ivanoff, Blaise van Hecke, Jane Downing, Kirk Marshall, Ryan O'Neill, A.S. Patric, Louise D'Arcy, Patrick Cullen, Erol Engin, Bel Woods, Les Zig, and a Foreword by Peter Farrar

Price: $20.00

Publication Date: 12 October 2016

Format: Paperback (216x140mm, 128 pages)

ISBN: 978-0-9953503-2-8

Category: Fiction

Take a journey into the minds of thirteen of Australia's most promising new and emerging writers as they delve into stories that explore the bonds of friendship and family, love and heartbreak, and coming of age and the loss of innocence.

Featuring A.S. Patric (winner of the 2016 Miles Franklin for *Black Rock, White City*), Ryan O'Neill (winner of the 2017 Prime Minister's Literary Fiction for *Their Brilliant Careers*), Emilie Collyer (acclaimed playwright), and many more, *13 Stories* is a bold, fearless anthology that's sure to offer something for every reader.

Lose yourself in the world of the short story, and revel in the craft of these talented authors – names you're sure to see more of in the future.

The Book Book

12 Steps to Successful Publishing
Author: Blaise van Hecke
Price: $15.00
Publication Date: February 2014
Format: Paperback (181x111mm, 148 pages)
ISBN: 978 0 992432 50 8
Category: Nonfiction

Everyone has a book in them, but where do we start? *The Book Book* breaks the process into manageable steps, providing tips, insider knowledge, and the inspiration to get your book published!

The Launch Book

The Little Guide to Launching Your Book
Author: Les Zigomanis
Price: $12.00
Publication Date: April 2015
Format: Paperback (181x111mm, 70 pages)
ISBN: 978 0 99243250 8
Category: Nonfiction

You've written a book but don't know what to do next. This simple and fun guide will show you how to have a great launch and celebrate your book coming into the world.

Pinion Press is an imprint of Busybird Publising, specialising in publishing a handful of our own titles yearly, trying to combine quality and enjoyability with some altruistic outcome, e.g. raising awareness for a particular condition (as our glorious coffee table photography book, *Walk With Me* – a journal of Kev Howlett's trek up to Mount Everest Base Camp and back – raised awareness of Charcot-Marie-Tooth disease), and/ or donate a portion of proceeds for books to various foundations (such as Women Helping Women, Breast Cancer Victoria, the Prostate Cancer Foundation, the Epilepsy Foundation, Vision Australia, and the Indigenous Literacy Foundation.

Busybird Publishing is a boutique micropublisher based in the heart of Montmorency, Victoria.

We help authors self-publish. A fee-for-service self-publisher, we make no claims on rights or royalties, and are determined that to make sure our authors have a pleasurable, gratifying, and educational journey.

We also run workshops on various forms of writing (fiction, nonfiction, memoir), publishing, and photography, and an annual two-day writing retreat; host a monthly Open Mic Night (the third Wednesday of every month); and hold competitions to help aspiring writers get published or win mentoring.

To learn more about Busybird Publishing, check out our website at **www.busybird.com.au**.